AVALON
BOOK OF BEASTS

WRITTEN BY TRACY BLOM

Contents

Introduction

Thousands of years ago, dragons roamed the Earth, their powers unparalleled by any creature. Three of these beings were called the Great Watchers: one with scales of fire, one with scales of ice, and one transparent. The ice dragons claimed their stake in the north, where glowing auroras made their scales shine like emeralds. The fire dragons sought the warmth of the jungle and flourished in tropical lands, and the third found refuge in a lake tucked deep within a piney forest.

The arrival of humans was the beginning of their end.

The humans couldn't hear the dragons speak when they tried to ask why. They hunted in the north, and they hunted in the south, thinking they got them all—but they were wrong.

CHAPTER 1

Beasty

For as long as I can remember, the war of beasts and fairies has existed, and if you trace it back far enough, you can find a single item at its source—a crown.

The beasts believed it belonged to them, as did the fairies, but because they could not come to an agreement, something else was done.

The Games of Magic and Might began as a challenge between a fairy and a spider. The fairy challenged the beast to a dual and even let the spider choose the location. Being a spider, it naturally chose the place it favored most—a single silk thread strung between two bean pods. The fairy quickly agreed, knowing she could use magic to fling the beans inside the pod and knock the spider off the thread. The fairies won that year, but the following year, the beasts sent another, far more intimidating creature: the fluffy bunny.

Bunnies, though adorable, are not to be trusted. Research any great heist in history, and you'll likely find a bunny nearby. Why? Because no one thinks to blame the bunny. It's too cute. Too nibbly. Too smart. The bunnies of Monoceros were perpetually known as great thieves and prided themselves on the matter. That year, and the following five, the beasts won.

As the years went by, the games became increasingly popular. Creatures traveled far and wide to catch a glimpse of the Magic Games; even the sea pirates of Andromeda came, which was impressive by both fairy and beast standards. Eventually, both sides forgot about the crown or why they were fighting at all; however, the war of beasts and fairies continued.

After years of watching magic, eventually, you learn how to do it yourself. No one would ever suspect a beast to learn fairy spells, which made my spell all the more exciting. Both sides blamed each other, but if they knew the real reason I did it, maybe they would understand.

You're probably wondering who I am.

I was born

of summer rain and soil,

rolled up in a web of morning sun.

I emerged with eight fuzzy legs wobbling beneath me as I took my

first steps, steps no one was there to witness. This was my first

lesson in independence; I needed no one to survive and preferred

it that way—until I met Jintao.

My name is Neith, and I am

A beast.

CHAPTER 2

Believing Is Seeing

Every story has two sides, and this one belongs to the fairies. It all began when I accepted an invitation to join my grandmother in the castle library for a day of reading tea leaves. The room, as I saw it, was ordinary, with towering bookshelves, little tables with vases of flowers on them, and a couple of chairs by the fire.

We took our seats as she poured the tea, and that's when I saw something strange—every shadow in the entire room was incorrect. The vase of flowers cast the shadow of a box. The bookcase cast the shadow of a knight, and the chairs we sat in had throne-like shadows, with tall backs and warped scepters on top.

I remember my voice quivering as I asked, "Grandma, is this really a library?"

She set the tea kettle on the table and answered, "Yes, Jintao. Why would you think otherwise?"

"It's just…" I leaned in with a whisper. "The shadows don't match."

She smiled before taking hold of my hand. "As fairies, we are born with abilities, some of which might seem frightening, but once you learn how to use them, you will understand why they are sacred."

A wave of magic swept over the room, revealing the true form of everything there. The bookcase now appeared as a display of armor, and the flowers appeared as a clear glass box with a glowing crown inside. Even our chairs changed into magnificently carved thrones with brilliant stones on the top. Only the tea remained the same.

"How did you—"

"Some things are better left as secrets. Do you understand?"

My eyes scanned the room of treasures, stopping on the crown. "What are we protecting them from?"

"Beasts."

I giggled. "Like the dog pigs and the racoonaphants?"

She shook her head as the leaves in her cup took the form of a beast with eight long legs dancing through the water.

Before I could inquire what it was, the leaves sank to the bottom, and the image disappeared.

"Why don't you go join the others?" she said. "Painting lessons are about to begin."

Every day, just after breakfast, the fairies gather for a painting party. The process begins with placing our easels at the foot of the statue we wish to paint. The colors and shapes that form upon the canvas come from how the statue makes us feel. Every day, a new creation is made, and once we feel like we've fully captured who they were, the painting is hung on the wall.

The teacher circled the room as we began to paint. "Now, close your eyes and envision the statue in its true form. What are they doing? Where are they going. Do they have kind eyes? Take what you feel from their presence and pair it with color."

There were many great statues to choose from—Cygnus, the bearer of the golden cross; Aquila, goddess of flight and incredible escapes;

and The White Tiger, one of the fiercest protectors to ever exist. Legendary beasts stood there, too, with Draco and Hydra among them. Most fairies gathered at the feet of Queen Lyra, wondering who might paint her best.

I, however, stood alone before the one empty pedestal, brush in hand, eager to paint who I knew was meant to stand there. I did exactly as the teacher instructed. I closed my eyes and pictured the creature who had charmed her way into my dreams. My brush slid across the canvas as I imagined her deep, red eyes shining like rubies and her long, dark fingers reaching for my light. With every brushstroke, I felt her loneliness. With my eyes closed, she and I were very much alike.

"What is that?" The teacher's voice echoed as my eyes flew open. Others gathered around, eager to look at the frightful painting.

"I....I don't know." I masked my excitement and mirrored their expressions.

The teacher pointed to the shadow of the reptile in the background.

"No, I meant that."

Before I could answer, my grandmother fluttered into the room, grabbed the painting, and stormed off.

"Grandmother, wait!" I hurried behind her. "I can't help it."

She spun around and wiggled her finger. "You can help it. Whatever has seeped its way into your mind has no business being there. Tomorrow, we work on protection spells all day!"

"Even the tea leaves know her name; eventually, I will, too."

Her cold blue eyes locked on mine before she disappeared. "Knowing its name will not make this any easier."

"Well, then what is she?"

"*It* is a beast named Neith."

* * *

Neith was born into the wild and lived among king snakes, Arctodus bears, and griffin flies, all of which became her closest friends.

Her gifts arrived in vibrant colors that spun from her fingers in grand designs. She created extravagant webs and hammocks that hung from the rocks overlooking the meadow. From there, she could see everything—racoonaphants roaming, unicorns grazing, and twinkles of fairies playing in the tall, green grass.

She kept careful watch of the fairies—not because she cared for them. Quite the opposite. Fairies were tricksters, always hiding things and able to disappear instantly. She didn't trust them and sometimes wondered what they tasted like. To be quite honest, she despised them, but the fairies seemed to be planning something, and she intended to find out what it was.

As luck would have it, Neith was relaxing in the coolness of a cave one day when a fairy happened to wander inside. She had long, brown hair and patterns on her skin like tree leaves. She smelled like rain and clover and twinkled with the essence of the forest.

Why a forest fairy was in a dark and dingy place like a cave was a riddle in itself. Neith closed her bright, red eyes and listened.

Nearly invisible footsteps approached as another fairy entered the cave.

"Hello, Jintao," the forest fairy said. "Hurry! This won't stay open for long."

Neith's eyes opened to slivers, spying a spinning portal of light that wasn't there before. On the other side, she could hear the sound of rushing water.

"What is this?" Jintao asked while reaching a hesitant hand towards the light.

The fairy whispered, "I'm building a world. Will you help me?"

The portal seemed less interesting compared to the newcomer. His wings held patterns of spiderwebs, and he smelled like mist and fire. For a moment, Neith wondered if he was a fairy at all. Something about him seemed different yet very familiar.

"What do you mean you're building a world? Does Queen Lyra know about this?"

"Of course she does; it was her idea."

Jintao stared into the light. "Why leave Monoceros when what we have is perfect?" he asked.

"A war is coming, and this new world will be our safe haven."

"How do you know?" Jintao asked.

"I saw it…in a simulation sphere," the fairy answered.

He laughed. "Simulations are not concrete. The thing you are planning for might not ever occur."

The forest fairy sighed. "Well, if it does, we'll be prepared. Now, come on. We have a lot of work to do."

Jintao paused before stepping into the portal. "What about the Aquatics? They won't be able to access a cave all the way up here."

"From what I was told, there is a ship for the Aquatics."

"What ship?"

The forest fairy shrugged. "That's Lumia's job, not mine."

The portal closed behind them, leaving Neith with only one thought: *If the fairies were leaving through the portal, and the Aquatics via ship, would the beasts be left behind?*

Drastic times called for drastic measures, so Neith did what anyone might do and cast a love spell on them all. With a little bit of luck and magic, the fairies and beasts would soon be close friends, ensuring no one would be left behind. That is, if she did the spell right.

Fairy magic is a fickle thing and can have horrible side effects if performed incorrectly. Neith saw no harm in attempting the love spell and believed that whatever might happen would be worth it so long as the beasts and fairies became friends.

She waited by the cave every day for Jintao. Sometimes, he would be gone for days, but one thing was for sure, he always had a present for her when he returned. They soon became fast friends, and even if she didn't go with him to the new world, it felt like she had. She counted the days in presents—seven pinwheels, ten origami spiders, three roses, one glowing moonstone, and a silk embroidered cloak. That's how long it took the fairies to build their new world.

"Neith, are you there?" Jintao asked while presenting the cloak. It glowed in the dark and had patterns on it like butterfly wings.

Neith's eyes flickered at the sound of his voice, and for a moment, she thought about eating him.

"There you are." He rushed to her side. "I made this for you. Here, put it on." He draped the cloak around her shoulders as she began to lift off the ground.

"What is this delightful contraption?" she whispered.

"It's so that you can fly with me," he gleaned.

The days that followed provided Neith with a whole new perspective. Sure, she had swung through the forest via web, but never had she been above the treetops. They flew behind waterfalls, through meadows and groves, and rode the wind until their hearts were full.

They settled into a nook on the cliffside to enjoy a nice dinner of mint and berries.

"This might be the best day of my life," Neith said while spinning a hammock for them to sit in. "Jintao, tell me about this new world."

"It's the most beautiful place you've ever seen, with waterfalls spilling over cliffs and groves of apple trees as far as the eye can see." His eyes lit up as he turned her way. "You know that piece of moonstone I gave you?"

She nodded.

"It's from the crystal caves of Avalon."

"Sounds magical," she said.

"It is! Very magical, actually. That moonstone is your ticket to Avalon."

She looked confused. "How?"

"Any time you want to be there, just hold the moonstone and think of the crystal caves."

"How will I think of a place I've never seen?" she asked.

"Hmm. Good point. Follow me. I think there's a way to show you."

They walked into the cave as he lit a small torch and held it up to the darkness. "Just give me a minute. I've never opened the portal by myself."

If there was one thing Neith knew well, it was shadows, and as the fire danced with his, she started to question what he was. His shadow changed from moment to moment, first into that of a reptile, followed by a spider and then a fairy. If she didn't know any better, she would think his shadow was confused.

"What's wrong with your shadow?" Neith whispered as it quickly lined up to match him.

"Nothing." He was quick to dismiss the question.

She saw right through his lies.

"Tell me what you are, or I'm leaving."

He sighed. "I'm a fairy. I told you. Hey, where are you going?"

Neith hurried off into the woods and climbed back into her favorite hammock.

Stars streaked across the night sky as she pinched the moonstone between her fingers and studied it. It could have been how the moonlight hit the stone, but for a moment, it appeared to be glowing. It pulsed within her hand as a strange feeling came over her, urging her to get to the beach.

She swung from the hammock into the breeze and rode a wisp of wind all the way to the shore. With the moonstone tight in her fist, she looked to the stars, where the constellation of an octopus glimmered. She watched for hours as it moved closer and closer to the ocean, and eventually, she fell asleep.

Jintao arrived at the cave before the sun came up when the rest of the world was quiet.

"Hello?" he called into the cave.

Neith's eyes flew open as the moonstone pulsed within her hand. She hurried back to the cave and crawled inside.

His steps, though careful, hurried towards her. "Neith? Is that you?"

"Yes."

He searched the darkness for her eyes. "I'm sorry about yesterday."

"Why won't you tell me what you are?" The hurt in her voice felt like his painting.

He exhaled deeply. "Because I'm still trying to figure it out."

"Well, maybe I can help you. Why don't you tell me about it?"

He paced the cave, wondering how much to share. "All fairies have shadows that are supposed to grow with them. Think of the shadow as an extension of the fairy that can help when they need it. For example, gold fairies' shadows can turn into giants, the red fairies' shadows can turn into weapons, and the forest fairies' shadows can turn into anything they want."

"Is yours confused?" Neith asked.

He laughed. "Seems like it. One minute it's a lizard, the next it's a spider—neither of which are fairy-related."

Neith laughed. "Maybe it wants to be a beast like me."

He perked up at the thought. "Speaking of beasts. Can you help spread the word that we leave tomorrow for Avalon?"

"The beasts are coming, too?" Neith smiled. Her spell had worked!

"Of course they are. We leave tomorrow at dawn."

"Oh, Jintao! This makes me so happy!" She threw her arms around him as a jolt of magic flew into her body. She pulled away and looked at her arms, which seemed to be flickering between invisible and visible. "What just happened? Why am I flickering?"

"It's probably just my fairy magic wearing off on you." He yawned. "I think I'm going to get some sleep. Big day tomorrow. Oh, and Neith, make sure to be here on time. The portal won't stay open for long."

* * *

A light mist filled the leaves with dewdrops, creating the perfect opportunity for a quick morning rinse. Neith slid down a silk thread, dipped her toes into the water, and then splashed it on her face. She gazed at her reflection, which should have been there, and screamed, "What's wrong with me?!"

She attempted to run, but something was throwing off her weight. A strange sack was attached to her body, making her slow and wobbly. She threw a web from her hands, attempting to swing to a nearby tree, and she sighed as it broke. She was far too heavy for a single thread, but maybe the cloak would work. She draped the cloak around her shoulders and flew towards the cave.

"Jintao? Are you here?"

The cave swallowed her words.

"Jintao? Something is wrong!" She ventured out into the forest, but it was eerily quiet, too. *The sun was shining. How was everyone still asleep?* Panic set in as she looked at the sun. It wasn't morning; it was mid-afternoon. She overslept!

She searched the trees for anyone to help, but no one was there. She went to the water to ask the Aquatics, but they were gone, too. *How could he have left her behind?!*

Suddenly, she remembered that the Aquatics had a ship.

"I have to get to that ship!"

She dipped one of eight toes in the water and quickly pulled it back. This was much deeper than the dewdrops in the leaf. She eyed the cloak, hoping it could carry her that far.

"Here goes nothing!" she exclaimed while jumping into the jetstream and flying up over the sea towards the tiny ship on the edge of the horizon.

She was nearly there when something strange rose up through the waves, with eight gigantic tentacles and glass-like eyes. This was a beast unlike anything she'd ever seen.

She flung a web towards the ship's mast and swung on board. Despite the roar of the ocean, she called to the Aquatics below. "Everyone, get to safety! There's a beast in the water!"

Eyes of terror met hers, reminding her what category she fell in.

"Beast!" an Aquatic screamed while pointing.

"They've got us surrounded!" shouted another. "Look! In the water!"

"No…I'm one of the good ones!" Neith ducked as a ball of magic whizzed past her head. Quick to get out of harm's way, she flung a web from her hands, swung around to the side of the ship, and crawled inside a nearby window.

A small child hid behind his mother, who glared at Neith like an angry mama bear.

"I guess the eight-legged beasts travel together. If Ophiuchus has sent you for the crown, we don't have it." The boat rocked as she grabbed onto the wall.

"Is that the name of the Octopus?" Neith asked while flinging a web towards the wall for her to hold onto.

"If you're not with him, then why are you here?"

"I'm looking for Jintao."

The child peeked between his mother's legs and answered, "Jintao stayed on Monoceros."

"What?" Neith's red eyes glowed with anger, scaring the boy back into hiding.

"He said he wouldn't leave without his friend. We waited as long as we could."

It was true. Jintao had searched high and low for Neith, but her use of fairy magic had turned her invisible, and he had walked right past her.

The ship rocked as they clung to the web.

"Stay here. I'm going to go get help!" Neith instructed.

"Are you sure that's a good idea? " The mother nodded towards the large sack attached to Neith's body.

17

"I can move just fine."

"But aren't you worried about your baby?"

"That's not what this is—is it?" Neith's eyes widened with fright. "Just stay here. I'll be right back."

Neith fired a web out the window and swung to the top of the mast, joining an Aquatic as the lookout. The golden patterns on her skin sparkled in the sunlight, and her wide eyes twinkled like stars as she gazed upon the glowing portal opening in the sky.

Neith placed a hand to her heart as her mouth fell open. Through the portal, she could see everything Jintao had helped create, the crystal caves, groves of apple trees, and waterfalls spilling over the cliffs. Even though he wasn't there with her, in that moment, it felt like he was.

"So, this is Avalon," the Aquatic whispered as the squid wrapped its tentacles around the ship.

Neith clenched the moonstone in her fist, imagining the crystal caves, and disappeared.

SABIK

Florenza, the sea queen, was a master of protection spells and keeping things hidden, which is why two extraordinary creatures fell under her care—Nirah, child of Ophiuchus, and a shapeshifting creature named Sabik.

No one knew where Sabik came from or even what he was. He emerged from a cocoon of fairy wings with two webbed feet and a piece of moonstone in his hands. The forest was brimming with life, yet no one was there to welcome him. He wobbled as he took his first steps, but just before falling, two brightly colored webs shot out from his fingers, holding him upright.

The shock of the webs scared him into a new form, with scaly skin, four short legs, and pointed teeth. Before anyone could witness his condition, he slithered into the water and disappeared.

Sabik found Nirah wandering the depth of the sea, collecting memories like seashells. Everything she touched became imprinted in her mind, and for years, she moved in silence like a little floating library, accumulating all there was to know. It was no wonder the two of them became fast friends. He could learn all there was about a place just by touching her hand, and she finally had someone she could call a friend. They didn't need to belong anywhere, and that was okay because the ocean was dark and deep and perfect for hiding them both.

By the time they turned the age of five, they had visited nearly every body of water on the planet. They rode the mist of hurricanes and sailed the waves of time, always returning to the sea queen to report all they saw. As the years passed, they yearned for more, and eventually, Florenza built them a home on Avalon.

She selected the perfect tree with winding roots that spread into the water. They could climb in and out as they pleased, and if ever they were ready to explore dry land, they could. It was a fortress of magic turned treehouse with trap doors, rope swings, and hammocks strung between the branches. They spent many great years here, living as one happy family.

"Nirah, where are you?" Florenza called from the tree towards the glowing lights moving through the forest.

"Coming!" she replied while chasing a golden fairy.

"I'm going to get you one of these days!" She swung at the fairy before falling on her face.

"Hey, you!" Sabik appeared out of thin air and jumped in her path.

"Ugh! Stop doing that!"

"What?" He smirked.

"Disappearing into everything! I feel like I have no privacy."

His eyebrows raised with judgment. "You're doing it again."

Nirah looked at her arms, which were glowing gold like the sun.

"So annoying. One day, I'm going to figure out why this happens, and then I'm going to fix it once and for all."

"Is that why you chase the gold fairies?" Sabik asked. "You think it's somehow their fault?"

"Partly," she said with a smirk. "And partly because I just can't stand them."

"I think they're nice."

"That's because you're part fairy," she said.

"Am not."

"Are so. Why else do you think you can disappear and fly, and—"

She glowed with envy as he laughed.

"How do you know?"

"Know what?" she scowled.

"Know that I'm actually disappearing or flying. Maybe I've been standing here all along and playing a trick on your mind." Sabik's eyes lit up as a chestnut fell from the tree. He kicked it toward Nirah's feet, temporarily halting their banter.

She kicked it back to him. "Well, whatever you're doing seems like fairy magic to me."

He flicked the chestnut into the air and bounced it off his thigh.

"You're magical, too, Nirah," he said while passing it back.

The nut rolled to a stop at her feet. "Glowing every time I'm mad isn't magic. It's a curse."

Sabik lowered his voice to a whisper. "Speaking of curses, I was swimming in the fairy pools this morning and heard a rumor. Apparently, the Aquatics used to be cursed."

Nirah laughed. "Cursed to be the kindest creatures ever?"

Sabik shrugged. "I'm just repeating what I heard." He began to walk away. "Anyway, see you later."

"Hey! Wait!" She reached into her pocket and pulled out a long silk thread. "I made this for you, so you can wear your moonstone instead of carrying it."

"Moonstone?" Sabik asked as she secured it around his neck.

She smiled. "You carry that stupid stone everywhere you go and don't even know what it is?"

He laughed. "I guess I never thought about it." He looked down, admiring the necklace. "Do you know what it does?"

She hesitated to tell him. "Kind of."

"Well, can you *kind of* tell me what it does?" He grinned.

She couldn't deny that great, big smile. "Different stones do different things." She nodded towards the moonstone. "That one is super special, and if you know how to use it, it can take you right to the Cliffs of Luna and some say to the crystal caves of Merlin."

"Who's Merlin?"

She sighed. "You're kidding me, right? He's only the greatest wizard ever to exist and a master mapper of the stars. You should try to use that moonstone and find him."

"Well, maybe I could get you a piece of your own and we could find Merlin together?"

Her eyes lit up. "Not only could we find him, but we could find any fairy carrying moonstone."

"Why would we want to do that?" he asked.

She shrugged, though her mind was filled with ideas. "In case you ever need to find any other fairies."

"I'm NOT a fairy," Sabik huffed.

"Mmm hmm."

"Hey, you want to drink tree sap later?"

She giggled. "Just like a fairy to love sweets."

"Do I look like a fairy now?" Sabik shapeshifted into crocodile form and slithered through the brush.

"Now where are you going?" Nirah called after him.

"Back to the fairy pools. It's a nice day for a swim!"

"UGH," she huffed in annoyance as a golden fairy buzzed by her head.

She swatted at it as another flew by, and then another.

"I wonder where they're going?" She followed them through the groves until she reached a tall golden gate with a beautiful garden on the other side. The fairies flew over as Nirah peeked her head through the shiny golden bars, spotting a castle.

"I don't remember there ever being a gate here." She touched the gate, zapping her finger. "Ouch!"

A unicorn emerged from the roses with its horn aglow. "That's because it wasn't there before."

He touched his horn to the gate as the spirals of gold came to life and continued growing around the castle.

"You built this?" Nirah asked in disbelief.

He bowed. "Sure did. The name is Uno."

Nirah's eyes narrowed. "Well, Uno, you're gate just zapped me."

He took a step back. "Sorry about that. It's designed to keep certain things out."

"Certain things?"

Uno took another step back. "Anything that might bring harm to the fairies."

"Ohhh, well that makes sense." She smirked. "Well, Uno, it was nice to meet you."

"Wait, I didn't get your name."

She called over her shoulder as she skipped into the woods, "Nirah."

CHAPTER 3

Exodus

S abik was enjoying the waters of the fairy pools when a strange whisper carried through the air. It sounded like a secret or a lie—possibly both. He lifted his eyes just above the water, spying two fairies sunbathing on a rock.

"You'll never guess who Uno saw today," said the one with brightly colored wings.

"Who?" asked the one with long, green hair.

"The child of…" she paused and looked around, "Ophiuchus."

The green-haired fairy gasped while placing a hand on her heart. "Here? On Avalon? I thought the sea queen had taken her far from here?"

"That's what we all thought. Apparently, she tried to get into the castle, too, but was zapped by Uno's gate."

The green-haired fairy leaned a bit closer. "Does she glow? You know, like her father did?"

She nodded. "The curse lives on. We need to tell the others."

The green-haired fairy looked around once more and whispered, "Does the beast have a name?"

She shuttered before answering, "Nirah."

Sabik dipped beneath the water and swam until he reached the sea. He floated weightlessly, letting the current carry him as he pondered what they said.

Sure, Nirah swatted at a fairy every now and then, but she wasn't bad. Nirah was his best friend, and if she was cursed, he would know it.

He was so lost in his thoughts that he forgot to pay attention to where he was going, which happened to be right inside a glowing sea cave. Colorful moonstone covered the walls and cast a purplish light upon the water, beckoning him to follow.

"What is this place?" he whispered while swimming towards what looked like a door at the end. It seemed like a secret passageway. Into what, he wasn't sure.

He made himself invisible, pulled the old iron handle, and slid into a hallway lined with torches. He thought about turning around for a moment, but then he heard voices. They seemed to be coming from a bright room at the end of the hall.

He crept to the door and looked inside, spotting two fairies in extravagant thrones seated before a roaring fire. One appeared ancient and wise and the other merely a child. His eyes widened as he gazed upon the objects displayed around the room, the armor of a knight, spheres made of crystal, and a glass box with a golden crown inside. The walls were covered floor to ceiling in books, one of which was titled *Beasts*.

"Do you hear something?" the child asked while looking towards the door.

The older fairy cast her gaze toward the shadow on the wall that looked like a reptile. This was a shadow she had seen before, long ago, in Jintao's painting.

"That's enough for today Severn. Why don't you go join the others in the great room."

The child gleefully skipped from the room as Sabik crept further inside. Every object seemed sacred and old, though not nearly as old as the woman. Her eyes followed his shadow as he inched into the room.

"You don't have to tiptoe around me. I know that you're here."

Sabik's feet locked to the floor.

"I assume you've come to learn about your father?" She grabbed her cane and smacked it upon the adjacent chair. "Here. Have a seat."

Sabik sat attentively, unsure if he should remain invisible or not.

As if reading his mind, she answered. "I can see you either way."

She looked to the book *Beasts*, then to a crystal ball that flew off the shelf and into her lap. She waved her hand over the crystal ball as sparks of magic swirled within, forming the picture of a spider.

"To learn about who you are you must first understand who your mother was."

Sabik watched in awe as the spider flung colorful webs from her fingers and swung freely through the forest.

"Neith was wild, dark, and free. A creature unlike any other. Much like yourself, she never knew her parents and spent many days alone." Sabik lowered his head, which she quickly raised with the tip of her cane. "Do not be discouraged. I believe that everything happens for a reason. With these lonely days, great courage came, along with independence, strength, and…well, something not even Neith expected."

Sabik gazed into the crystal ball, watching as the spider danced with silk and sunshine, creating hammocks and dreamcatchers. A male fairy entered the scene and wrapped a glowing cloak around her shoulders. She took hold of his hand, and together they flew.

"Who is that?" he whispered.

"His name was Jintao, one of our most gifted fairies." She chuckled under her breath. "They were the unlikeliest of friends, but they seemed to make each other happy."

The image changed, showing glimpses of their love story. Sabik watched with wonder as Jintao opened a glowing portal and placed a piece of moonstone at her feet.

"What happened to them?" Sabik asked while wrapping a fist around his necklace.

She exhaled deeply. "Well, your mother, though well-intentioned, dabbled in magic that she shouldn't have."

"A beast doing magic?" Sabik asked.

She placed her hand over the crystal ball, shielding the image within. "You see, beasts and fairies haven't always been so kind to one another, and when war came, your mother feared the beasts would be left behind. So, she did what anyone would do, and she cast a spell."

A burst of magic clouded the crystal ball as she pulled her hands away.

"Well, did it work?"

"Yes, but not in the way she had planned. While she successfully restored the beast and fairy friendship, her spell had great consequences and turned her invisible—among other things. So, when your father went to look for her, he couldn't find her."

The bottom of the crystal ball filled with water as a ship appeared.

"Thankfully, Neith remembered the fairies had a ship, but by the time she got there, it was too late. For everyone."

Tentacles rose through the waves and wrapped around the ship.

"At least they were together," Sabik said as a tear trickled down his cheek.

Silence loomed.

"They were together, right?"

She sighed. "Your mother was aboard the ship looking for your father, who refused to leave Monoceros without her."

Sabik glared at the crystal ball.

"That beast—the one who killed my mother—what was its name?"

"Ophiuchus."

That name. Why did it have to be that name?

It felt like his heart had sunk into his stomach as he struggled to speak.

"I—I have to go," he said while scrambling towards the door.

"Wait... Sabik...there's so much more to tell you!" she called down the hall after him. "Don't you want to know about your father— what he was?"

His mind spat questions at his soul as he ran through the forest towards home.

*Home…*his footsteps slowed as he scanned the trees. These were trees he had climbed with Nirah, trees he'd licked sap from and strung hammocks through. Trees he grew up in alongside *her*—the child of Ophiuchus.

His entire life had been—he struggled to find the words—a secret, a lie, a mistake. What he wouldn't give to disappear from it, and then he remembered that he could.

CHAPTER 4

A Whole New World

Nirah searched the sugary maple tree, fairy pools, and all of Sabik's favorite puddles, but he was nowhere to be found. She even went back to the castle to ask Uno if he'd seen him.

"What do you mean he's missing?" Uno said.

"I've searched everywhere. I even checked the fairy pools."

"*You*—checked the fairy pools?"

"You seem surprised." She glared.

"Well, you aren't exactly a friend of the fairies. Did anyone see you?"

"Strangely, no one was there."

"It's because they're all here." Uno nodded towards the castle.

"A meeting of fairies. Is something wrong?"

The unicorn lowered his head. "Someone opened the cave portal, and whoever it was went to the human world."

"Well, it couldn't have been Sabik. He loves it here on Avalon."

Uno cringed. "Well, he did, until today."

Nirah glowed like a ball of fire as she raced through the woods towards home. She grabbed a rope, catapulted to the top of the tree, and landed with a thud in the kitchen where Florenza was fixing a meal of honey beans.

She panted, trying to catch her breath as Florenza rushed to her side.

"Nirah, honey, what's the matter?"

"Sabik…he left Avalon."

Her eyes widened to the size of saucers. "What do you mean he left Avalon? How?"

"There's a portal in a cave, and somehow he opened it."

She set the beans down and paced the room. "Why would he leave? Did something happen?"

The hurt in Nirah's eyes spoke for her. "Is it true? Am I the child of a monster?"

She wrapped her arms around her. "Oh, dear. I planned to tell you about this one day when you were much older."

"If you're not my mother, then Sabik isn't my brother?" Tears spilled down her cheek.

"I raised you to be strong, noble, and good. Your father may have been a monster, but you are not."

Nirah's lip quivered as she glowed a bit brighter. "Sabik left because of what I am…and what my father did to his parents."

Florenza grabbed her by the shoulders and looked her square in the eyes. "We are going to get him back because we're family, and that's what family does."

"How will we find him without any powers?" A glimmer of hope returned as she remembered the moonstone. Maybe she could find him that way.

Florenza cast her gaze to the forest. "We will save him together. It's time to call a meeting of beasts. Tell those you know to meet at Summit Rock."

* * *

A circle of stones surrounded a central pillar where Florenza stood, waiting to address the crowd. The meeting commenced as beasts entered—first, the black wolves, followed by Arctodus bears, racoonaphants, dog pigs, and cheetahs, all of them eager to bring Sabik home.

"Thank you all for coming. As you may have heard, one of our very own has gone missing. We believe Sabik opened a portal, which he used to travel to the human world."

A stir of whispers swept the crowd as Florenza continued. "Now, I know that the human world is off limits, but desperate times call for desperate measures."

The black wolf stepped forward and bowed before speaking. "We've tried to exist in the human world, and it always ends badly. They hunt us, trap us, and view us as enemies. It isn't wise to venture there."

The ground shook as Ursa, head of the bears, stepped forward. "The wolf is right. We all know what happened to the dragons—and the unicorns."

A noise came from the brush as Uno peeked his horn through.

"Speaking of unicorns," Florenza smiled, "it's nice to see we have the unicorns' support."

He emerged from the bushes alone. "Well, you have mine."

She nodded. "Very well. Now, for those who are coming with us, I thank you, and for those who stay behind, I understand. You should know that I would do this for each and every one of you because we are beasts, and beasts stick together."

The wolf stood beside her. "Like a pack."

She nodded. "Like a pack—and where one goes, the others follow."

The wolf howled towards the sky as the others joined him. "The wolves are in."

The bears exchanged worried glances. "If the wolves are going, the bears will go, too."

The calls of the wild sounded one by one as the beasts rallied around Florenza. All eyes turned to Nirah, who stood alone.

The black wolf growled, "And what say you, child of Ophiuchus? Will you join us?"

She nodded, but deep down, she knew that if she were to help, she would need powers, and she knew just where to get them.

CHAPTER 5

Vega

Sabik stood inside the mouth of the cave and watched as the rain poured down. From what he could see, the human world wasn't *too* different from Avalon. Trees surrounded him, and rain, and—hmm, that was funny. He couldn't hear anything speaking. He paused, noticing how quiet it was. No bells of fairies, whispering wind, laughing beasts—all was quiet in the woods. He perked up at the sight of a maple tree.

"Delicious sap, here I come!" He attempted to pierce the tree with his claw but smacked his hand instead. "Ouch!" His eyes widened as he looked at his—hand?!

He raced through the forest toward what sounded like rushing water and stopped abruptly at the edge of the highway. Boxes sped past with humans inside, one of which nearly hit him.

His breath quickened as he stumbled backward, and suddenly, he fainted.

"Hey? You okay?" A spunky red-haired girl poked his shoulder with a stick as he opened his eyes.

As much as he wanted to tell her how much he wasn't okay, he nodded. "Where am I?"

"You're in the Pines." His face remained unmoved. "You know, Pine Barren forest?" She extended her hand and helped him to his feet. "You must be new around here. My name is Vega, and these woods are known as the Pines. Anyway, my mom is fixing chili for dinner, and no offense, but you look like you could use a good meal."

He nodded while thinking, *what's chili?*

They walked through marshy bogs, past winding streams, until they hit the trail head.

"What are you doing out here anyway? You know, it really isn't safe to be in the woods by yourself."

Sabik scanned the trees, spotting a cardinal, then a squirrel, neither of which seemed scary. "It doesn't seem unsafe to me."

She laughed. "Maybe not right now, but wait till the sun goes down." She stopped walking for a moment as her eyes widened. "This is the home of the New Jersey Devil…and trust me, there have been lots of sightings in these woods."

His lack of response evoked a sigh. "Tell me you've heard of it?"

He shook his head.

"What's your name?"

"Sabik."

"Well, Sabik, the New Jersey Devil is a monstrous beast with hoofed feet and dragon-like wings that only comes out at night." Her eyes grew bigger with every word.

"Why are people scared of it?"

She laughed. "Did you hear what it looks like?"

The trees parted, revealing a small gravel path leading towards a two-story home. Vega smiled at the sight of her stepmom, Alice, who was seated on the back porch wrapped in a heap of blankets.

"Dinner is inside on the stove," Alice said with a smile. "Your friend is more than welcome to join us."

Sabik sloshed a pile of chili into his bowl and took a seat. He stared at the brown concoction and decided it was best only to eat what items he knew—beans, tomato, green onion. The weight of their stares caused him to set his spoon down.

Sabik smelled the air, attempting to read the room. Alice smelled like lavender and some other strange smell he couldn't identify. Whatever it was made him sad.

"So, Sabik, Vega says you're new around here," Alice said before coughing into her napkin.

"Yes, that is correct," he answered.

Vega nudged him to keep eating. "It's better hot."

He spooned out a few more beans.

"Something wrong with the chili?" Vega's dad Wes asked. He was a stern man with cold eyes and stains on his hands—the type you can't wash off. He smelled like chemicals and secrets.

Sabik sat a bit taller. "No, the beans are delicious."

Wes scowled. "So, Sabik, where did you and your parents move from?"

Sabik shook his head. "No parents."

They exchanged troubled glances.

"What do you mean, no parents?" Alice said. "Sabik, honey, are you living in those woods?"

He nodded. "Yes, where else would I live?"

That answer triggered even wilder stares. "In a house. You know, like this one."

Vega gently nudged Alice under the table. "Maybe Sabik could live with us for a while. I don't mind sharing my room."

Alice looked to Wes, who sighed. "You think that's a good idea?"

Vega was quick to answer. "I've been sleeping in the treehouse anyway. He can have my room."

"Treehouse?" Sabik perked up.

Vega flashed a smile. "Yep! Once we finish dinner, I'll show you."

Colors of pink and gold covered the sky as the sun began to set. Sabik and Vega raced through the yard towards the treehouse, alerting the fireflies with every step.

"This is how I get up," Vega said while climbing the wooden ladder attached to the tree. "There's also a rope, or—" she stopped mid-sentence, shocked to see Sabik already at the top. "Wow, you're a good climber."

"I've had a lot of practice."

Together they sat on the highest branch looking out to the forest. "You want to hear a secret?" Vega asked with a serious stare. "I've seen the New Jersey Devil."

"Really? What did it say?"

She looked at him half-crazy. "It didn't say anything." She handed him a set of binoculars. "Here, look through these and tell me if you see the lake."

He pressed them to his face and nodded.

"This was right around the time that I saw it. I was sitting here, just like this, and this dinosaur-looking thing with spikes on its back stuck its head up from the water."

"But it didn't say anything?"

"What? No. Why do you keep asking that?"

"Not everything has to speak for you to hear what it has to say." He lifted the binoculars towards two heaping smokestacks. "What's that?"

"Oh, you must be talking about the factory. That's where my dad works."

"Works?' Sabik asked while scanning the windowless building.

Vega laughed. "Yeah, you know, like a job where you make money. My dad is a scientist and researches stuff."

Sabik squinted as a strange green glow came from the trees beside the factory. "Hey, I think I see something, and whatever it is, it's running towards the lake!"

Vega snatched the binoculars and scanned the trees. "I don't see anything!"

"Are you looking at the lake?"

She looked towards the water just as something green dipped beneath the surface. "What was that?" She lowered the binoculars and turned towards Sabik.

"Green Devil?"

"New Jersey Devil," she corrected. "And first thing tomorrow, we're gonna find it."

CHAPTER 6

Taken

Nirah hid near the top of the waterfall and waited for a young fairy named Bruxo. He arrived every day like clockwork, leaf in hand, ready to ride the waterfall's mist. He was good at surfing, but then again, who wouldn't be with a magical, floating leaf? She had been tracking him for days and had actually stumbled upon his morning routine by accident.

Unbeknownst to him, he had buzzed right past her head while she was getting a drink of water and nearly knocked her into the pool. She swatted at the golden fairy, chased him to the top of the waterfall, and was just about to pounce when she saw the piece of moonstone dangling around his neck.

He teetered on the leaf as the moonstone pulsed with light. The moonstone flickered as he rolled his eyes.

"It's like they know I'm trying to have fun. Why do they always need something every time I'm surfing?" He removed the necklace and set it on a rock. "Whatever it is can wait."

Nirah crept through the brush towards the stone. Stealing it didn't seem like it would bother Bruxo too much; if anything, he might thank her. She'd only use it to locate Sabik, and once she was done, she'd give it right back.

***

What was supposed to be a gathering of beasts turned out to be a party of two. Florenza nervously scanned the brush. "I'm sure more beasts are coming. Just give them a few more minutes."

A golden glow radiated from Nirah as anger fumed. "I knew it. You heard the black wolves; everyone's scared of the human world. No one is coming."

Florenza sighed. "Okay, then we move on to plan B."

"Which is?"

"Us."

Nirah laughed under her breath. "Do you even have any powers? What are you going to do, make them a nice meal?"

Florenza's eyes narrowed. "Just because you haven't seen my powers doesn't mean they don't exist. After all, I protected two of the most powerful creatures on Avalon all these years." She muttered under her breath, "Think I don't have powers."

The mention of powers sparked another question. "What can you tell me about my father? What powers did he have?" Nirah was quick to beg. "Please, Florenza, if I inherited powers, I deserve to know what they are. Maybe it will help us find Sabik."

She exhaled deeply. "There's no kind way of saying what your father was. He was a squid, capable of sucking the powers from all that he touched. He was dangerously greedy and rumored to be in love with a female pirate. She was the only thing more ruthless than he, so he sailed the seas of time following her pirate ship."

Nirah laughed. "An octopus in love with a human?"

Florenza shrugged. "Stranger things have happened. He was a master escape artist and busted her out of prison a time or two. They were friends—strange, thieving, pirate friends."

"What happened to them?"

"The pirate uncovered a crystal that opened doorways in time, allowing her to steal precious goods in every era. He lost sight of her for a while and returned to the stars to rest. When her ship emerged without her on it, he reacted the only way he knew."

Florenza's voice trailed into the background as Nirah imagined such power. *If she were as powerful as her father, whose powers would she go after first?*

"And that was the ship Sabik's mother was on," Florenza said, returning Nirah's attention to the present.

"How do you know all of this?" Nirah asked.

"Because I was on that ship, too, along with the aquatics and centuries of gold and treasure."

Nirah's eyes widened. "Gold?"

Florenza smirked. "Let's just say that's why you're a golden child."

"Do I want to know what happened to my father?"

Florenza shook her head. "I think our time would be better spent devising a plan." She walked towards a boulder, picked up a rock with a pointed edge, and began drawing.

"Now, the cave with the portal is located here." She marked the spot with an X. "Which I believe can only be opened by a fairy."

Nirah cringed while unfolding the moonstone from her hand. "Does this help?"

"Do I even want to know where you got that?"

"Let's just say I did Bruxo a favor," she replied with a triumphant smirk.

Florenza resumed drawing. "Now, one of us should stay and guard the portal while the other slips into the human world and finds Sabik."

They spoke in unison. "Good, you stay here."

"No, Nirah, it is best that I go. I'm his mother, after all."

Nirah schemed in silence. "You're right. Let's meet by the cave first thing in the morning after we've had a good night's sleep. I'll stay behind."

That night as Florenza slept, Nirah crept through the forest visiting those whose powers she wished to acquire. She went to the dog pigs first, whose power, unbeknownst to her, was horrible breath. The smell nearly knocked her unconscious. So far, she was off to a terrible, stinky start.

As she stole the powers of the Arctodus bear, she could feel her muscles convulsing, teeth growing, and her sense of smell heightened. It was as if she could smell everything within a hundred mile radius, making her horrible breath even worse. Maybe she should have started with the wolves. She crept to their den and was met by the green eyes of Zuma.

"Nirah? What are you doing here?"

She could feel his power seeping through the darkness—a power too strong for her to take. "I—I wanted to see if you'd join us. No one else came."

Zuma stepped to the edge of the den. "Maybe no one else came because they knew you would come for them first."

She averted her eyes. "I don't know what you mean."

"Yes, you do." The points of his ivory teeth glared. "And if you've come for my powers, then you've come for a fight."

Nirah slowly backed away. "Do you find me so foolish?"

Zuma cringed at the smell of her breath. "Foolish enough to steal dog pig powers."

"Clearly, I need your help, and still, you refuse."

"I'll tell you what. If you've not returned in seven days, the beasts will come to your aid." He narrowed in on her. "On one condition."

"Name it."

"Return the powers you've stolen to their rightful owners," he sneered. "If you're anything like your father, this will prove to be a challenge."

"I'm nothing like him." She stormed off in a golden flurry.

CHAPTER 7

Slime

By the time Vega woke up, Sabik had already gone to the lake, tracked the strange prints in the mud, and collected a sample of hydrodictyon. Vega gave a cat-like stretch, cracked her back, and reached for the binoculars that were covered in slime.

"Eww! What did you do to my stuff?" She grabbed the only clean part of the binoculars and flung the web of green goo to the treehouse floor. "What is this?"

He beamed with excitement. "It's a poly-structured, highly regenerative freshwater organism from the lake! The new cells mirror that of the parent cell and separate off to form webs of their own once the parent dies."

Vega's face twisted with question as she uttered only a sound, "Huh?"

"It's algae."

She sneered at the slime-covered binoculars. "And how did it get on my binoculars?"

"So, this morning it was really foggy, and I couldn't see a thing. So I went down to the lake to see if I could find the Green Devil—"

"New Jersey Devil," Vega corrected.

"Right. Anyway, I was down by the lake when suddenly, a set of steps came up out of the ground and—get this! Not one, but four of them ran up the stairs and into the lake!"

"Funny…but for real, what did you do to my binoculars?"

"I tried to catch one of the lizards, but it was covered in algae and really slippery. I slipped, then the binoculars slipped, and you know the rest."

Vega laughed. "You expect me to believe that? You lie as much as Eddie."

"Who's Eddie?" Sabik asked.

Vega sighed. "Someone I probably shouldn't hang out with but do. You'll probably meet him someday." She questioned the statement as she said it. "Maybe that's a bad idea."

"Why?"

"He's jealous sometimes." She reached for the stack of comic books in the corner and stopped at the sight of more algae. "I see you like comics."

"What's a comic?" Sabik answered.

She held her favorite comic book up to eye level as slime dripped from the pages. "It's basically a story of heroes and villains, and most of them have superpowers."

He thought of Nirah. "Are any of them born without powers but get them later?"

Vega nodded. "Lots of them. That's what makes comics good."

Sabik nodded towards a comic book with a hand-drawn cover and unfinished pages. "What's that one?"

Vega's eyes lit up with excitement. "I'm writing my own comic!" She hurried to grab a stack of flashcards. "And making my own playing cards, too. See this one here, this is Midge, she's like a firefly, nature fairy thing. She's mean and feisty but has a soft spot for nature and plants. You wouldn't want to mess with her because she has magic powers that can erase your memory."

Sabik nodded towards the next card depicting a white bunny. "Who's that beast?"

Vega looked half offended. "He's not a beast! This is Sambu, the warrior bunny." She tilted her head, admiring her drawing. "There's this mysterious old man I see around town sometimes with long, white hair and a bunny that's almost the same color white. He kind of looks like a wizard, and he inspired this card."

"Bunnies are marvelous tricksters where I'm from."

Vega laughed. "Oh, yeah? What else happens where you're from?" Vega grabbed her pencil and hovered over the blank page, eager to draw his story.

"Well, basically, every year, there is a battle of beasts and fairies called the Games of Magic and Might. Nowadays, it's pretty playful, but long ago, it was pretty serious. The beasts believed that the fairies stole a crown that belonged to them, and so they played these games every year to see who would hold onto it."

Vega's pencil scrambled across the page as she hurried to draw what she thought was a beast. Sabik intervened, "Oh, and the beasts have a team of magic horses called unicorns. Some of them, like Uno, can create golden gates with their horns."

Vega quickly sketched a horn and swirling gold gate. "Uh huh. What else?"

He hesitated to tell her anything more. After all, no one outside of Avalon had ever heard these stories, and some of them weren't his stories to tell.

"Well, unicorns get really hungry, and it turned out they ate all the food in the land. So, they sent some of the creatures here to the human world to find more."

Vega lifted the pencil and paused. "Sent from where?"

Sabik lowered his voice in case the trees were listening. "Avalon."

Vega smirked. "Like the Avalon in the King Arthur and Merlin stories?"

Sabik looked shocked. "You—you know Merlin?"

Vega leaned in with a stare. "Everyone does. He's a legend. People have been talking about Merlin for like a thousand years."

Sabik paced the tree house, stopped, and then resumed pacing. "That's not possible. Merlin and his bunny are alive on Avalon."

Vega didn't quite know what to say, and instead, she returned her attention to the cards. "Want to see my third favorite card? It's Lark, the telepathic raven."

"Tele-what?"

Vega laughed. "It means that she delivers messages to people through thoughts. She's a good friend to have." She spread all three cards out in her hands. "Which one do you like the best?"

Sabik pointed at the bunny.

"You seem like a warrior bunny type of guy. Here. You can have it." She tucked the rest of the cards into her back pocket, closed the comic book, and placed it back on the shelf. "Oh, and don't worry about getting slime on the cards. They're laminated."

"I don't know what that means, but I trust you," Sabik said.

"But if you do feel bad about the comic you slimed up, you can buy me another one for my birthday."

"Birthday?" he questioned.

"You know, birthday like the day you were born. People bring you presents and stuff to celebrate. My best friend, Barb, always gets me a chocolate torte from the coffee shop she works at. That reminds me." Vega pulled a glowing rectangle from her pocket, tapped it a few times, and whispered, "I'm calling Barb to remind her about the party."

The glowing rectangle made a strange purring noise. Then, a voice came from the other end. "Hey, this is Barb. I'm probably doing something super sciency that would only bore you if I picked up, so I didn't, and you're welcome." *Beep.*

Vega sighed. "Hey, Barb, it's Vega. I'm having a party this weekend at the skating rink and bringing my new friend Sabik. You guys can totally nerd out together over algae and science stuff. P.S. don't forget the torte. Just kidding. But really, don't forget it. Bye."

She tucked the rectangle back into her pocket and resumed the conversation as if everything was normal. Sabik's frightened eyes said otherwise.

"What was that?" He nodded towards her pocket.

"What, my cell phone?" She pulled it back out of her pocket as he flinched.

"It's just a phone. You know, to call people on." She extended it his way as he shuddered. "See? It's not scary at all."

He remained frozen until she put it away. "Anyway, if you want to get me a new comic for my birthday, you can, but comics cost money, and if you don't have a job, then you probably don't have money. On second thought, how about you just come to my party. That is all the present I need."

He took off his moonstone necklace and handed it to her. "How about this? Can this be my birthday present?"

She looked genuinely shocked. "I… this is too nice. I don't even —" she studied the rare stone. "Where'd you get this?"

He smiled. "Avalon. Now you have something to remind you of me."

She attempted to hand it back as he pushed it away. "I insist. Just like I insist I saw lizards running out of the ground into the lake."

The moonstone pulsed with light as she secured it around her neck. "Giving me presents doesn't make you sound less crazy."

He nodded towards the binoculars. "And that green goo you're so scared of is the same stuff that was on your dad's shirt. Let's just ask him about it and settle this once and for all."

"No!" She grabbed his arm. "There's only one rule in our house; don't ask dad about work."

"What are the rules about exploring the factory?"

Vega was quick to answer. "There aren't any."

"Good. Let's go have a look around."

* * *

"I seriously can't believe we're doing this," Vega muttered under her breath as they crept along the side of the factory. Every crunching stick or sound caused the cringe on her face to deepen and the flashlight to wobble.

Sabik plucked the flashlight from her hands. "Here, I'll go first. I can see really well in the dark."

"Thanks." She trailed behind him as her face relaxed. "So, what exactly are we looking for?"

Sabik slid his fingers along the cement wall. "Some kind of clue that connects the algae in the lake to what was on your dad's shirt."

Vega halted her steps. "This seems like a really bad idea."

He spun around to face her. "Look, I know that you didn't see what I saw, and spying on your dad seems wrong, but something in my—" he placed a hand to his heart and paused, looking for the proper words.

"Heart?" Vega questioned.

He giggled. "Why would my heart have feelings?"

Vega smirked. "This is a *whole* other conversation. We'll talk about it tomorrow after my—" Shock froze on her face. "Oh, no. I have a huge test tomorrow that I haven't studied for! Sabik, I really hate to do this, but I need to get home."

He looked at the path ahead and then back at her. "I'll just have a quick look around and be home before you know it."

* * *

The next morning, Vega threw on her backpack, grabbed a banana, and headed for the treehouse.

"Hey, Sabik, you awake?" She climbed a few rungs and peeked inside. "Sabik?"

She scanned the empty room—blankets neatly folded, comics put back in place, and a heaping basket of foraged chestnuts. "Impressive."

Maybe he got up early and was somewhere in the woods. She had to walk through the woods anyway to get to school; maybe she'd find him there.

"Sabik? Are you here?" she called to the trees, but the forest was eerily quiet. No chirping birds or morning crickets. Even the wind seemed still. She placed her hand to her heart as a strange heaviness set in. Something was wrong.

That night, Sabik didn't come home for dinner, either. Vega stared across the table at the green blotches on her father's shirt as questions pinballed through her mind. *Did Sabik make it inside the factory, and if so, what secrets did he find? Were the answers to those questions hidden in the blotches?*

"Vega?" Alice motioned towards the plate. "You haven't touched your food. Something on your mind?"

She twirled spaghetti around the fork. "Uh, no. I mean, yeah." She glared at her dad. "It's just that Sabik didn't come home last night, and I haven't seen him all day. Have you?"

Wes gave a quick "nope" before shoving another bite in his mouth.

As much as she wanted to scream *you're lying* she didn't, and she excused herself from the table instead. She felt bad for abandoning the meal she knew Alice spent precious energy cooking and paused with one hand on the door.

"Dinner is great; it's just that I can't eat right now." The moonstone necklace tugged her out the door.

"Vega, honey, where are you going?" Alice went to stand as her legs quivered, forcing her to sit back down.

Vega called over her shoulder as she headed into the woods. "We're the only family Sabik has. Somebody has to look for him."

"Please try to be home before sundown!" Alice called after her.

Vega walked through the woods, retracing their steps to the factory. By now, she sounded like a parrot calling the only word that it knew. As she said Sabik's name for the eleventh time, something strange caught her eye—a giant thread of iridescent silk clinging to a nearby tree. Her eyes widened as a beam of sunlight passed over it, casting a kaleidoscope of color upon the forest floor.

"What kind of spider made that?" Vega whispered while reaching a curious hand towards the web.

The side door to the factory flew open as she instinctively grabbed the web, which flung her to the top of the tree like some kind of superhero. In an effort to silence her screams, she covered her mouth, inconsequentially sealing her lips with a web of pink. Try as she might to pull it off, it remained resilient, battling her every move.

To make matters worse, she now had company. A frazzled woman wearing a white lab coat hurried out of the factory, eagerly looking for someone to talk to. She settled for herself.

"Just go in there and tell them you quit. Say it exactly how you rehearsed. There's science, and there's ethics and this—"

The door flew open again as a stocky man with a wiry mustache came out.

"Seriously, Wendy? Another break?" His stare lingered.

 "Yeah, Wes, I'm taking *another* break because what we're doing in there is—crazy."

He cringed. "About that. You're going to want to get back in there. That thing you found, it's kind of—gone."

"Gone or disappeared? There's a difference." She hurried back inside as Wes scrambled after.

The heavy door began to close as Vega jumped from the tree, attempting to catch it. *Please don't shut!*

As if in tune with her thoughts, the pink web flung from her lips, wrapped around the doorknob, and held it open.

"If I didn't know any better, I'd think you were trying to help me." She slid into the darkness and lingered in the hall. As much as she wanted to call out for her dad and scream a laundry list of accusations, she didn't. Instead, she stood there and took a deep breath.

"Okay. Think, Vega. If Sabik were here, where would he have gone?"

The pink substance suddenly seemed to glow, rolled itself into a ball, and bounced in excitement. "What are you?" The closer she leaned, the brighter the ball became. "You can't understand me, can you?"

The ball suddenly melted into a puddle, reflecting her face. "Very funny. You think I'm talking to myself?"

The puddle remained stagnant.

"If you want to know my name, it's Vega."

The goop excitedly rolled into a ball and bounced.

"Oh, I see. This is a game or something?"

The ball bounced again. "Okay, so, do you know where Sabik is?"

The bright pink ball lit up as it bounced off the walls and ceiling. Vega covered her head and giggled. "Okay, okay. I take it you've seen him."

The ball melted into a sticky puddle around her feet, making it nearly impossible to move. "Hey, what'd you do that for?" The more she struggled, the firmer it became. "Knock it off. I'm really stuck here!"

The glowing goop returned to ball form and bounced with excitement.

"Is Sabik stuck here?"

It bounced again.

"Can you take me to him?"

The ball bounced down the hall as she hurried after.

"Hey, wait for me!"

The factory was like a labyrinth of hallways lined with fluorescent lights and closed doors. Vega slowed her steps as she approached the end of the hall. She could hear voices coming from around the corner, from an area that sounded large and echoey. She leaned in, trying to assess a familiar yet calming sound. *Is that water?*

The sound of rushing water was instantly drowned by voices— Wendy, the woman from outside, her dad, and two others.

"Trust me. It is in the room. It's just that you can't see him. Try kicking a soccer ball his way. For some reason, the kid can't resist and will kick it back to you."

Did she just say kid? Vega peeked around the corner and scanned the height of the room. Everything was blindingly white, from the shiny marble floors to the hive-like ceiling overhead. Something about it reminded her of the dentist—cold, sterilized, and able to cover painful acts without much notice. What she couldn't figure out was where the sound of water was coming from. She looked to the pink goop for answers, but it was already halfway across the room, attempting to pry open another door. Vega watched in amusement as it tugged at the handle, slid into key form, and jimmied open the door.

The scientists dispersed as Vega made a mad dash towards the open door and slid inside.

"What is this place?"

It was like she had stepped onto a movie set with lush greenery, trickling waterfalls, and heavenly mist that smelled like plants. A butterfly fluttered past and landed on a strand of winding jasmine.

"What would paradise be without butterflies?" she joked while kneeling to study the strange creature with purple wings and patterns of abstract gold upon them, or was it green? She squinted toward the changing patterns on its wings. "Never seen a butterfly like you before."

"That's because I'm not a butterfly, and those aren't wings. It's a cloak."

Vega jumped, nearly falling into the pool as she looked for the source of the voice. "Who said that?"

"Up here," the voice called from the pink web strung between two rocks, "in the hammock."

Vega tilted her head back. "Who—or what—are you?"

The hammock gently swung side to side. "I've been called many names—beast, spider, AHHH—but you can call me Neith."

"Nice to meet you, Neith. I think."

"And nice to meet someone crazy enough to sneak in here." She swung from the hammock down to the floor, her shimmering cloak on full display with eight hairy legs beneath.

"Ahhh!"

"I told you to call me Neith. Ahhh is fine, too, I guess. Anyway, we don't have much time in here unless you want to end up like one of them." She nodded towards the pool where tiny green orbs of light flittered in the water.

As Vega leaned in, she could hear the sound of bells ringing at different levels. "What are those things?"

Neith's eyes filled with sadness as she gazed into the water. "Can you hear them crying?"

Vega nodded. "You're starting to sound like Sabik."

"So you *have* seen him?" Neith asked.

Vega's eyes remained locked on the tiny green lights. "Well, not since yesterday. He's been staying with my family. Long story short, he thought something fishy was happening here, and it looks like he may have been right."

"Oh, these aren't fish; they're fairies. Elementals, to be exact. How they got here, I haven't a clue."

Vega's eyes widened as she stared at the flittering lights. "Did you just say these little swimming lights are fairies?" She reached into her shirt and pulled out the necklace.

"I think this thing is making me crazy."

Neith stared at the necklace like a long-lost friend.

"Where did you get that?"

The stone buzzed like a streetlamp in a lightning storm. Neith reached a careful hand towards it, and suddenly, Vega felt the elementals' sadness, pain, and fear—all at once.

A tear trickled down her face as she tucked the necklace back into her shirt.

"It was a gift."

The sound of approaching footsteps caused them both to freeze. Vega scanned the room for somewhere to hide as Neith shot a web towards the ceiling and disappeared into the rafters.

Vega whisper-screamed towards the ceiling. "Real nice. Way to leave me down here!"

The footsteps drew closer as a familiar voice echoed from outside. Seeing no other option—get caught or jump in the water—Vega took the plunge and opened her eyes. The water was crystal clear, remarkably deep, and much more than a simple pool. It was an underwater world connected to other habitats, or in this case, enclosures. Behind the glass door to one enclosure was a group of underwater dogs, swimming effortlessly without coming up for air. Vega looked to the next pane of glass, where a herd of brontosaurus-like creatures waited eagerly for their turn to enter the pool, and then there was a room that held no water at all, resembling a doctor's office. Vega swam towards the glass and looked inside. There was a doctor's chair, jars filled with colorful liquid, a desk with papers scattered about, and…*what is that?*

Vega pressed her hands to the glass as something inside pressed theirs to hers. Something she couldn't see but could feel. The moonstone necklace pulsed with light as Sabik's voice floated into her mind.

"Vega? How'd you get in here?

Sabik? Is that you? Why can't I see you?

"Because I'm invisible, but I can't stay this way forever, and eventually they'll find me again, and the tests will continue.

Don't worry. I'm going to get you out of here! Did you say tests? And how are you in my mind?

"They're studying me, taking samples, and making serum of some kind. And I don't know how I'm in your mind, but I am.

This is what my super raven Lark does! Sabik, you're a superhero! Speaking of powers, somehow I don't feel like I need to come up for air. Is something wrong with this water?

"Remember that algae I was talking about? There's something in the water that has to do with super cells. I don't know how, but they replicated so many times that everything is affected."

Oh, my gosh. I have to get you out of here. How do I do that?

"See the jar of blue liquid on the shelf behind me? It is the only way we can leave here together."

He suddenly pulled his hands away as the door behind him opened.

Vega's eyes widened as her dad entered the room, grabbed the jar of blue liquid, and left.

"You have to get that serum! In the wrong hands, it could be really dangerous…"

Vega swam to the surface to catch her breath as a strange suction pulled at her feet. She shoved her head back underwater and watched with fright as the cage to the Brontosaurus enclosure opened. The giant lizards paid her no mind and gleefully swam towards a sudden opening in the wall. It looked like a circular piece of metal cut into pie-like slices that had swiveled open, revealing a giant waterslide behind it. One by one, the lizards surged into the tunnel as Vega hurried after, slipping and sliding down a very long, watery shoot.

"What in the!!!" Vega pressed her arms to the walls, attempting to brace herself for the end of the tunnel and the quickly approaching lizard's butt. She smacked right into it as it farted in her face.

"Geez! Do you mind!?" She cringed as it looked over its shoulder, smiling like a happy dog as it marched up the stairs into the piney forest.

Before she could wrap her mind around where she was, the lizard farted again and disappeared into the lake.

"Unbelievable," she whispered as the electronic stairs retracted back into the ground as if they were never there at all.

CHAPTER 8

Monster

By the time Florenza realized what Nirah had done, it was too late. She had stolen the powers of what creatures she could, fled through the portal in the cave, and was halfway through the Pines.

Using the bear's super smell, Nirah followed what she thought was Sabik's scent until the forest ended and a maze of towering skyscrapers began. The closer she got to the city, the stronger the smell became. It seemed to come from all directions—dark alleys, sewers, and streets. Her senses were firing on all cylinders as she raced down the closest alley and stopped in front of a strange metal bin. She tore back the lid, shocking even herself as she did it, and glared at the contents within.

Her bear-like instincts celebrated the stinky prize while the realist in her frowned.

"Stupid bear powers led me to a heap of trash!" She shoved the lid closed and fired a glare towards the end of the alley, where a stocky kid stood watching her. His unicorn t-shirt was half-tucked in, and his eyes had a slight upwards squint. His body reminded her of star-jelly, wiggly and weird.

She had never seen anyone like him, yet she felt she knew him. Even stranger was the shiny pink sports car parked behind him with a silver dragon on the hood.

The back door to a coffee shop swung open as a teenage boy covered in tattoos came out holding a bag of trash.

"Hey, you better not be digging in our trash. You hear me?" He flung the bag into the metal bin and lingered in the doorway.

He lit a cigarette, took a few puffs, and tossed it at her feet. "I better not catch you out here again."

His smoke-filled smile widened as he turned his attention toward the kid in the unicorn shirt.

"Hey loser, is that your weird pink car?"

His laughter ceased as a girl emerged from the coffee shop with short, bobbed hair, thick, clear glasses, and a knee-length purple dress. He stood a bit taller in her presence and stopped talking.

"Really, Eddie? Picking on someone with special needs? That's a new low for you."

"Whatever, Barb. You're lucky I don't pick on you."

The kid at the end of the alley shuffled away as the pink sports car followed. Nirah slid behind the dumpster, hoping Barb and Eddie wouldn't notice, but they did.

"Awe, look! Dumpster girl is scared," Eddie laughed.

"And yet she smells better than you," Barb smirked as Eddie rolled his eyes.

"Whatever. I smell good. Nerd."

"Well, this nerd just got a scholarship and a full ride to college—the same college where your girlfriend Vega will be going this fall." She tilted her head with an exaggerated sulk. "Oh, you didn't know? Sorry."

He stormed inside and yelled over his shoulder. "She's not my girlfriend anyway."

Barb peeked behind the dumpster. "It's safe to come out. Eddie can be such a jerk sometimes." Barb's eyes softened as she assessed the out-of-place stranger—tangled hair, a strange leaf-covered dress with trash sticking out of the pockets, and what could have been the worst breath she had ever smelled.

"Hey, I don't know your story, and I'm not judging, but if you'd like something to eat, I'd be happy to buy you lunch and maybe loan you some clothes."

Nirah's stomach growled as she smiled.

"I'll take that as a yes." Barb held open the door as the smell of coffee wafted through the air. "I'm Barb, by the way."

Nirah's eyes lit up as she spotted a lone bean on the ground, plucked it from the floor and ate it. The look on Barb's face made her feel wrong for doing it, but the taste in her mouth said otherwise.

"We don't usually eat things off the floor here," Barb said with a forgivable grin.

"Oh, I don't mind," Nirah replied. "That was delicious!"

Barb steered her towards a table and pulled out the chair. "You can sit here if you want. I'll be in the kitchen making you something to eat. Does a sandwich sound good?"

Nirah restated the new word, "Sandwich."

"Okay, cool. I'll be right back."

Moments of solitude allowed Nirah to assess her new surroundings. People seemed to come from all over to delight in the bean juice and waited in an endless line for it. Back on Avalon, when you had something delicious, you always shared it, but here, people were very protective over their bean juice, and once they got their cup, they scurried off to enjoy it alone.

Was the bean somehow in control? What powers did it have?

She looked around for watchful eyes before picking up another bean and placing it on the table.

"What are you?" she whispered. It didn't answer…not yet. She lifted her eyes and scanned the room, noticing the long line of people obediently waiting for their cups.

Somehow, this simple bean had caught them. But how?

Her gaze lingered a bit longer, assessing each person in the room. Every single person except for an older man with long, white hair holding a tiny white bunny had a piping hot cup of—

"Coffee!" Barb said while setting the cup on the table. "There's cream and sugar over there if you want it. Oh, careful. It's hot."

Nirah angled her face, trying to find the white-haired man, but he was gone. Barb followed her line of sight, looking at the empty chair.

"Something wrong?"

Nirah took a sip and paused, assessing whether or not she loved or hated it.

Barb ran to get the cream and sugar. "Here, try it with this."

Nirah dumped the entire sugar upside down as Barb winced. "I don't think you need that much. Here, let me get you a new one."

Nirah took another sip as molecules of precious energy bounced through her body. She wrapped her palms around the cup and pulled it closer. "No, this is great. Thank you."

"Glad you like it." Barb paused. "What's your name?"

"Nirah." She took a sip of coffee followed by a long exhale.

The smell of her breath caused Barb to take a few steps back. "I'll be right back with your sandwich."

Nirah savored every bite of ham as if it were her last meal, though something about eating it felt wrong. She licked her fingers and combed them through her hair, causing Barb to make that face again.

"You know, I'm off work in five minutes and would be happy to show you around town. I'm assuming you don't know anyone here?"

Nirah momentarily stopped combing grease through her hair. "Sure, and maybe you can help me find my friend, Sabik."

Barb's mouth hung open. "Sabik? Why do I know that name? Hold on." She reached into her apron and pulled out her cell phone, replaying Vega's voicemail. "It looks like your friend Sabik is staying with my friend Vega. Small world, huh?"

* * *

Barb and Nirah stood on Vega's back porch and knocked on the door. To their surprise, a chipper Alice greeted them. Her typical layers of warm clothes were nowhere in sight, and her skin held a vibrance that no one, including Alice, had seen in years.

She eyed Nirah's strange, leaf-covered outfit. "Hi, Barb, and—who's your friend?"

Barb sniffed the air. It smelled like fresh-baked cookies inside. "Uh, this is Nirah. We met at the coffee shop. Smells good in there."

Alice raised her eyebrows and nodded. "Thanks. I just made a batch of snickerdoodles. You gals want to stay for dinner? I'm making red pepper and sausage spaghetti."

A loud crash came from upstairs, causing everyone to jump.

Barb craned her neck and looked behind her. "Everything okay in there?"

Alice seemed somewhat embarrassed. "Don't mind Wes; he just lost something, that's all. I'm sure he'll calm down before supper."

Barb couldn't help but admire Alice's glowing skin. "Well, I hope he finds it, and in case no one's told you today, you look beautiful."

Alice smiled, despite the series of crashes coming from inside. "Thanks Barb. That's very sweet of you. Anyway, you kids want to come in or—"

Nirah cocked her head like a bird, homing in on Alice's golden glow. It was strangely familiar, yet—

"Impossible," Nirah blurted.

Alice sighed. "I know, it is kind of impossible right now with all of this racket going on, and I hate to break it to you, but Vega isn't home, either, which is strange since it's nearly dinner time."

Barb jumped in. "We're actually here to see your houseguest, Sabik. Is he around?"

Alice jumped as another crash came from upstairs. "Sorry to say Sabik *was* staying with us, but unfortunately, we haven't seen him for a couple of days now."

Wes marched halfway down the stairs and screamed, "Where is Vega?!"

Nirah ducked behind Barb as Alice turned to face him. "Wes! Do you mind? That is no way to act in front of our guests."

His face turned red as a tomato as he stomped back upstairs. "Well, she's the only one who could have taken it!"

Alice quickly stepped onto the porch and closed the door behind her. "I haven't seen Vega since this morning, but if I had to guess, I'd say she's either in the tree house or the woods."

"Or at Eddie's," Barb said under her breath.

Alice perked up at the foreign name. "Who is Eddie?"

Barb stumbled over a failed response. "Uh, he's no one from the coffee shop."

"And just where does this *no one from the coffee shop* live?" Alice's mouth hung open as a shiny pink sports car rolled into the driveway. She squinted towards what appeared to be a vacant driver's seat and shook her head. "Is that one of those self-driving cars, or?"

All eyes turned to the car as it revved its engine. Barb looked at Nirah, who was walking in a trance-like motion towards the vehicle.

"Nirah? Where are you going? Do you know them or something?"

Another crash alerted Alice to the door. "I'm sorry I couldn't be of more help. I better get in there and help him before he tears the house apart."

Before she could retreat into the house, Barb asked, "What exactly did he lose?"

Something held her tongue as she looked away. "Just some medicine. Oh, and Barb, try to be indoors before sundown. There's been a lot of bats around here lately."

* * *

"Are you following me?"

Nirah stood in front of the car and crouched down to eye level, coming face-to-face with the hood ornament—a silver dragon with ruby-red eyes. It reminded her of a story Athena told her when she was a child about an ancient dragon with eyes like fire who disappeared, quite literally, from the human world to ensure dragons' survival. No one really knows how he did it, nor did he tell. Some say he stole a crystal with magic powers far beyond the reach of time. Others say he met a chameleon who taught him a thing or two. Whatever the case, it was because of him that dragons live on, earning himself the name "Transparent One."

She slid her fingertips along the shiny hood, feeling the growl of the engine. It shook through her being like thunder, and for a moment, she wondered if there was a way to take such power.

"Don't even think about it." A voice snapped her to attention. Nirah pulled her hands away. "Who said that?"

Silence lingered. *The raspy voice sounds much older than me.*

"Yeah, but I don't move like it." The voice replied with a laugh.

"Who are you?" Nirah spun around and scanned the yard.

The sultry voice whispered just loud enough for her to hear. "An old friend from Avalon. Now, get in."

69

Nirah looked to the treehouse where Barb's search for Vega had taken a detour towards her comic book collection. Nirah sighed. "Humans spend their time on the strangest things."

"And you're wasting just as much time standing out there."

Nirah glared at the car. "You can talk?"

The sassy car replied, "And drive, too. Now, get in. I think I know where Sabik is."

The car rumbled with laughter as Nirah slid into the driver's seat.

"What's so funny?"

"That you think you're driving."

Nirah smirked. "Someone has to, right?"

The car sighed. "You can sit wherever you like, but I'm still in control." Nirah slid into the passenger seat as the car rolled down the driveway.

Barb scrambled to put the books away and poked her head out of the treehouse. "Hey! Nirah! Where are you going?"

The window rolled down without her touching anything. "To go find Sabik."

Barb eyed the vacant driver's seat and fired off questions. "You know where he is? Is he at Eddie's? Whose car is that?"

The window rolled back up as the car horn played a farewell jingle and sped down the street.

"So...old friend from Avalon, do you have a name?" Nirah's eyes scanned the car's interior. Everything was shiny and black—black seats, accessories, and a giant screen in the center playing a video of clouds. The faster she drove, the faster the clouds passed by. Every move she made was mimicked on the screen, prompting her question. "You're not *really* a car, are you?"

The radio turned on, playing the sound of chirping birds and wind sweeping through the treetops.

"Hey, I know that sound." Nirah closed her eyes as the arms of the forest wrapped around her mind. "That's Avalon."

The car replied, "If you listen closely, you can hear the echo of my cave."

Nirah's eyes fluttered open. "You're a dragon?"

Nirah's eyes widened as she drove right through a stop sign. "Hey, dragon, I think you're supposed to stop at those red things. All the other cars do it."

"Well, I'm not every other car, am I?"

Two flashing lights came from behind as Nirah hopped into the driver's seat. "Oh, no. Just stay quiet and let me do the talking."

"Fine."

The cop tapped on the window as Nirah hit every button, trying to roll it down. The cop's frown deepened as the radio turned up and the sunroof opened.

Nirah popped her head out of the sunroof and gave an awkward smile. "Sorry, my thing isn't working."

The cop placed her hands on her hips. "By 'thing,' you mean window or ability to stop?"

Nirah laughed under her breath. "Window."

The cop pulled a pad of paper from her front pocket and began writing. "Do you know why I pulled you over?"

"We didn't stop at the red thing."

Something about that answer caused the cop to lower the booklet and stand up straighter. "You mean the stop sign?"

"Yes, lady."

"That's Officer to you." She tapped her name badge. "Officer Height."

"Sorry. Officer Height."

The cop pressed her pen to the paper. "Now, you said, 'we didn't stop,' which makes me think you aren't alone. Is someone else in the car with you?"

Nirah rattled off the only thing that felt honest. "I normally have my best friend with me, but he's missing, and I didn't stop at the stop sign because I'm not in control."

The cop's brow furrowed as she pulled the pad back out. "Did you say someone's missing? How long has your friend been gone?"

She seemed eager to write down whatever Nirah had to say.

"His name is Sabik. He's about my age, and he loves sweet stuff and playing kick-nut." The cop's pen lifted from the page again.

"Did you say kick-nut?"

"You know, the game where you kick a nut back and forth."

"Ohhh, like soccer?"

Nirah shrugged.

"So, when was Sabik last seen?"

Nirah's head swiveled towards Vega's street. "He's been staying with a family that lives at the end of that street. Apparently, he's been sleeping in their treehouse, but he hasn't been there for a few days." She exhaled. "To tell you the truth, I'm relieved. Between the shouting and throwing of things, I can't imagine he was happy there."

The cop's curious factor increased by double. "You saw all this? What were they yelling about?"

Nirah shrugged. "Vega's dad lost something and was upset, which must have rubbed off on his wife because her skin was glowing. Mine does that, too, sometimes when I get mad."

The cop bypassed that statement and went on to the next. "This friend of yours—Sabik—does he have a home to go back to?"

Nirah nodded. "Of course he does. On Avalon. But, sometimes he disappears, making him hard to find. That's the fairy in him, you know?"

Her sunglasses slid down the tip of her nose as she stared into Nirah's eyes. "Are you messing with me? Look, I've had a long day, and if this is some made-up story to get a rise out of me, then—"

The car lurched forward, sending Nirah toppling through the sunroof.

"What are you doing?!" the car grumbled. "Stop talking about Avalon!"

A furious knock came at the window. "Open this door right now!"

Nirah sat back and watched the evolution of the cop's emotions—concern grew into impatience, which morphed into anger. It could have been her bear-like senses, but the angrier the cop became, the more she could tell about her. Even from behind the glass, she could feel the woman's heart rate quicken and smell traces of what she ate for lunch. She could feel her lack of sleep, which impacted her ability to act as quickly as she used to. It seemed there were a lot of things she couldn't do as well as she used to.

Nirah placed her hand on the window and took a deep breath. This woman wasn't tired; she was sick with the very same thing that Alice was.

The window slid down as Nirah reached a careful hand towards the woman's heart.

"What are you doing?" The cop flinched as Nirah placed a hand on her chest.

"If I take your pain away, you'll have more energy, and if you have more energy, you can help me find Sabik."

"What do you mean—take my pain? How do you—"

Before she could finish, a jolt of energy surged through the woman's body, and as she exhaled, Nirah inhaled all of her sickness, fear, and pain all at once.

"What have you done to me?" cried the woman, staggering backward. "What are you?!"

Clouds of darkness floated into Nirah's eyes as the cop hurried back to her squad car and called for backup.

The car had something to say about it, too. "What did you just do? Are you crazy?!"

Nirah gripped the dashboard as her vision began to flutter. "I don't know! I—I'm having trouble seeing!"

"Because you have literal shadows in your eyes! Her troubles were not yours to take! I have never seen anything like this in my years of existence. There has to be a way to fix all this. Think, Athena, think!"

"Athena?" Nirah questioned.

The car dipped down an alley and headed for the shipyard. "You were going to find out sooner or later. If you haven't guessed, creatures from Avalon aren't exactly welcome here. This disguise was the best way to keep me safe. At least, that's what Florenza thought."

Florenza's name was a reminder of her guilt. "Did Florenza come here, too?"

"No. She stayed behind in case we needed help getting home. Same with the wolves."

"We? Who else came here?"

Athena pulled between two shipping containers and turned off her headlights. "Let me think, which creatures didn't have their powers stolen? Me, the hamsters, Uno, and the bears."

Nirah cringed. "Actually, I took the bears' powers."

"Well, you missed Ursa's husband, and boy, is he mad. Anyway, we have bigger problems right now. How are your eyes?"

Nirah carefully stepped out of the car and turned towards the ocean. "All I see is darkness."

Athena sighed. "Shame you can't see that beautiful sunset."

A tear trickled down Nirah's cheek. "Probably not as pretty as the sunset on Avalon. Now that's something worth watching."

Athena rolled to the edge of the pier and looked across the bay, spotting a carnival.

"Speaking of lights, just across the bay is the most fantastical thing I've ever seen. It's like a spinning wheel with colorful lights all over it." She revved her engine. "That's Officer to you just need light! Get in! We'll have your vision back in no time."

CHAPTER 9

Fairies, Wizards, and Beasts! Oh, My!

Officer Height tapped on Vega's front door and waited only a moment before walking to the backyard. She climbed the ladder to the treehouse and looked inside, spotting a stack of comic books and a bin full of chestnuts.

"Kick-nut," she laughed while plucking a chestnut from the pile and tucking it in her pocket. She quickly examined the rest of the treehouse, searching for anything that looked out of place. "Do I even want to know what this is?" She snarled at the algae-splattered binoculars and slid them into a plastic bag.

"Who's up there?" Wes called towards the menacing flashlight. "You have five seconds, and then I'm calling the cops."

She peeked out of the treehouse. "No need. Already here. I'm looking for a missing child. Goes by the name of Sabik. You seen him?"

Wes scowled. "Sorry to say that kid's long gone by now. Kids like him come and go, you know what I mean?"

She folded her arms and lowered her chin. "No. I don't know what you mean." She climbed down the ladder to meet him.

"No offense, it's just that kids like him don't usually stay in one place for too long, and given this town's record of disappearing kids, I'd say it's unlikely you'll find him."

She angled the flashlight towards his chest, highlighting the familiar green splatter. "Just because he's homeless doesn't mean he doesn't matter. All those kids matter, which is why I keep looking for them."

Wes sighed. "Look, all I know is that my daughter befriended him, and he spent a couple of nights in our treehouse."

"And this daughter of yours, is she home?"

Wes began to pace. "Uh, no. I don't think so."

The door swung open as Alice stepped onto the porch. "Wes, everything alright?"

Officer Height blinked a few times, trying to shake the vision before her. "Ma'am, are you… glowing?"

Alice blushed. "You have to forgive me. I know this sounds strange, but I—I'm on this new medicine that—"

"Alice, why don't you get back in the house," Wes grunted.

The two women made momentary eye contact before she retreated inside.

"As I was saying. You won't find him here. Now, if you don't mind, my wife is on some medicine and needs to be looked after."

Officer Height paused before leaving. "Thanks for your time. I'm sure we'll be seeing each other again."

* * *

On the other side of town, Barb was busy scaling the side of Eddie's house, trying to get Vega's attention. Climbing wasn't really her strong suit, but the garden lattice provided enough of a ledge so that she could look inside the window. She peeked inside, spotting Vega sitting on the bed.

Being a natural fidgeter, Vega couldn't help but dig into her pockets and pull out her playing cards.

"What I wouldn't give to fly out of here right now," Vega whispered while staring at the card depicting Midge.

Barb ducked as Eddie stomped into the room, looking angry as ever.

Vega shoved the cards into her coat beside the stolen serum. "Well, you're looking pleasant this evening, Eddie. Maybe we should do dinner another time."

He slammed a drawer or two and paced the room. "Depends on how you answer my next question."

Vega seemed unamused. "Oh, is that what it depends on? Not if you're nice to me or get your act together?"

His eyes narrowed in on her glimmering necklace. "I'll cut to the chase. I heard that you've been seeing someone else. That true?"

Vega laughed. "What? No."

He got right in her face and glared at the necklace. "Then what's that?"

A deep gulp proceeded her words. "Just calm down, Eddie. It was a gift. For my birthday. You know, the one you missed." She tucked the necklace into her shirt and walked to the window, momentarily locking eyes with Barb.

She spun around, hoping Eddie hadn't noticed, which he hadn't. He was too busy taking his frustrations out on the old TV set. He slapped the side as a picture appeared between fuzzy lines.

Together they watched in shock as a stampede of well-dressed hamsters raced across the screen. He slapped the TV again, hoping it was some kind of a fluke.

"Are those hamsters...wearing clothes?" Vega walked like a zombie toward the TV. "And is that a bear...in a business suit? What show is this?" She turned up the volume and listened as the frantic reporter went on about the oddities.

"To those of you at home who just witnessed this bizarre series of events, there's only one word to describe it: a circus. Authorities are on the move trying to figure out just where these adorable, dapper animals came from and how to hopefully get them back to wherever they belong. This, coupled with the absurd number of bats emerging from the forest, has everyone on high alert."

Eddie rolled his eyes, yanked a towel off the doorknob, and walked out into the hall.

"Where are you going?" Vega yelled. "Don't you want to see this?"

"To take a shower. I need a moment to think about you and your birthday present!" He slammed the door behind him.

The sound of rushing water was Vega's cue to leave. She hurried to the door and pulled. "Locked? Are you kidding me?" She raced to the window and tried to slide it open, but it wouldn't budge more than an inch. "Ugh!"

Barb peeked her head up, nearly scaring her half to death.

"Barb! You have to get me out of here! It's a long story, but I stole a magic serum from my dad's work, and I need to get it back to Sabik. Oh, and Eddie is mad about a gift Sabik gave me and—"

Barb jimmied the window a little more, trying to open it. "It won't budge. Is there any other way out of here?"

Vega looked to the door and then back at Barb. "Not without crossing Eddie."

"Well, what about that magic serum? What does it do?"

Vega shook her head. "No way. I promised I would bring it back to Sabik."

Barb leaned in with a whisper. "Well, how much is in there?"

Vega held the bottle up. "Not much."

The water turned off as both girls locked eyes. "Well, maybe just try a drop and see what happens."

Vega could hear Eddie slamming doors and muttering to himself in the hall. "I guess I could just try a drop."

Barb nodded. "And I'll be right here if you need me. If anything happens, I'll find a way to distract him."

Vega stood in front of the mirror, plopped a drop into her mouth, and swallowed.

For a moment, everything seemed fine, but then it was as if time slowed down, and she could feel every living thing like it was a part of her—the dying plant in the corner, the smell of impending rain, and a strange pulse that came from her necklace. The pulse was more like a phone call from someone else's mind, but when she picked up, all that answered was darkness.

Despite the darkness, something was there—something very much alive. She inhaled the smell of the ocean and the familiar sounds of the boardwalk, taking her back to childhood memories soaring high above the world on the Ferris wheel. She took another deep breath and opened her eyes, expecting to see her reflection, but it was gone.

What's wrong with me?

What should have been her reflection appeared as a speck of fluttering gold zipping through the air.

"Who said that?" A voice called out from the dark place in her mind. *"Is someone there? Sabik, is that you?"*

Vega flew around the room in a chaotic spiral, trying to look at the wings attached to her back. "What am I? And who's saying that?!"

Panic instantly transformed into fear as Eddie burst into the room and looked around.

"Vega? Where'd you go?" He stomped through the room. "I did some thinking in the shower, and you know what I think?" He dropped to his knees and looked under the bed. "I think you're lying. So, why don't you tell me about your new boyfriend and where you got that necklace?"

The voice fluttered through Vega's mind. "Sabik's necklace? Are you with Sabik? Tell him this is Nirah!"

"If you want to find Sabik, go to the factory!" Vega yelled, though her miniature scream sounded only like an annoying buzz to Eddie. He stormed downstairs and out into the yard.

Vega flew towards the window, spotting Barb's car parked on the street.

"Oh, no! Barb!"

Thankfully, there seemed to be a teeny hole in the screen, a hole just big enough for her to fly through.

"Here goes nothing!" Vega closed her eyes, flew through the hole, and out into the open air.

The smell of rain intensified.

"Oh, no."

An army of heavy drops fell from the sky as Vega zipped between them and headed towards the open window of Barb's car, which she was just about to roll up.

"Barb! Wait!" Vega flew toward the crack but collided with a giant raindrop as she toppled inside.

Barb's careful eyes followed the golden speck like a cat chasing a laser. "What kind of bug are you?"

"I'm not a bug! I'm a—I don't know what I am, but we have to get out of here!"

To Barb, her screams sounded like a tiny, high-pitched bell. Eddie trudged across the yard just as Vega returned to regular size, materializing in the seat beside her.

"Ahh!" Barb screamed while flooring the gas pedal. "Vega?!" Barb swiveled her head between the open road and her glowing friend. "What's wrong with your skin?! You're glowing, gold, like—"

"Alice," the girls said in unison.

"Are you okay? Where'd you come from?" Barb's face seemed frozen in a state of wide-eyed shock.

"That serum I took, it turned me into—" she held her tongue, unwilling to say what she knew she was—what Sabik was.

"A bug?" Barb hooked a left and drove towards the coffee shop.

Vega took offense to the comment. "A fairy."

Barb laughed. "Do you have a magic wand now? Where is it? Can I see it?"

Vega rolled her eyes. "Real funny."

"Well, how'd you get back to normal size?"

Vega's eyes followed the windshield wipers. "The rain." She suddenly wondered if that's why Sabik was the only prisoner not held in an underwater cave. *If he got wet, would he grow, too?*

"Anyway, where are you going? My house is that way."

"You honestly want to go back to your house right now?"

Vega paused. "Yeah, I bet my dad is pretty mad that I stole that serum. You know, Alice has been feeling so much better lately, like how she was before the cancer." Vega gasped. "Hey, when I found Sabik he said something about them running tests and trying to find super cells. Do you think they are trying to develop a cure for cancer or something?"

Barb did a quick U-turn. "No wonder Alice's skin was glowing! She's been taking that stuff!"

Vega laughed. "I think I'd know if my mom—I mean stepmom—was a fairy."

"Alice is basically your mom," Barb took hold of Vega's hand and lovingly squeezed. "And maybe that serum impacts people differently. Whatever the case, we can't just barge into your house and confront your dad about it."

Vega's eyes remained on the road. "We're going to have to confront him eventually. He has Sabik locked away in the factory, along with his other 'test subjects.'"

"You think you know someone," Barb said.

Vega sighed. "Had I known that Alice was taking it, I—"

Barb glanced over at her. "Don't blame yourself for this. It isn't fair. As much as you want Alice to get better, this is not the way to do it."

Vega nodded. "You're right, which means there's only one thing to do. Sneak back into the factory and return the serum to Sabik."

Barb seemed pensive and quiet.

"Something the matter?"

Barb turned into the woods and drove towards the factory. "I just feel like I can't help you much. What I am supposed to do, make a chart about it?"

Vega laughed. "You are really good at data science." She perked up. "That's it! Why didn't I think of it before? What if while I am freeing Sabik, you sneak into their fancy office and access the computers? That way we can find out what they are *really* up to."

They did a mini-high-five. "Okay, I'll drop you off at the factory, head to their fancy office, download what I can, and then come back to get you."

***

Athena drove across the bridge towards the glowing lights of the carnival.

"Can you see anything yet?" Athena asked.

Nirah shook her head. "No, but the strangest thing happened. I saw a light come into my mind, like a tunnel connecting me to someone else. She could hear me, and I could hear her."

"Her? Who was she?"

"I—I don't know, but she knew where Sabik was and was carrying his moonstone." Nirah suddenly remembered the moonstone she had stolen from Bruxo and clasped it in her hand.

"Very strange," Athena said. "Why would Sabik give away his moonstone? He cherished it."

Nirah laughed. "He didn't even know what it was until I told him."

"Still, the boy cherished it because it came from his mother."

"It did?" If Athena had eyes, Nirah would have stared into them. "Did you know Sabik's mother?"

"And his father—both spectacular creatures. Father part fairy, mother part—" Athena paused, trying to find the correct label. "It is because of his mother that the worlds of beast and Fae united."

"It sounds like she was a wonderful woman."

Athena pulled onto the boardwalk and parked between two food trucks. "What do you mean was? As far as I know, Neith is still alive."

With those words, a flash of light shone in Nirah's eyes, allowing her a momentary glimpse of the Ferris wheel but not the people on it. She creaked open the car door and waited.

"She's still alive? Well, this changes everything! Oh, Athena, this means more than you can possibly know!" Nirah got out of the car and waited. "Aren't you coming, Athena?"

"My two forms in this realm are talking car and dragon, neither of which belongs here. Take only what you need from the light, and when your eyesight returns, hurry back to the car."

Nirah hurried toward the Ferris wheel, and though she was certain no one was following her, it sure felt like someone was. She had felt this way since the alley where she first saw Athena and the boy in the unicorn shirt.

She walked past the line of people and dipped beneath the rope.

A voice called out behind her. "Young lady? You have to get in line and wait your turn."

His voice faded into the background, and all she could hear was the power she sought—buzzing through conduit, crisscrossed around the wheel, and blinking in tiny bulbs that seemed to call her name. Athena's instructions to take only what she needed faded into that same background, and as she placed her hand to the Ferris wheel, she drained it of all that it had with one deep breath.

The boardwalk went dark as screams rang out, along with pointing fingers and orders for her to freeze. Lightning buzzed from her fingertips and shone bright as the moon in her eyes, and suddenly, she could see the fear on everyone's faces.

"Monster!" someone yelled as Athena sped down the boardwalk toward her.

"Nirah! Get in!" Nirah sprinted towards the car and yanked open the door. The very touch of her electric hands short-circuited Athena, causing her car headlights to flash, radio to blare, and sunroof to open and shut.

"Athena?" Nirah screamed. "What's the matter? Are you okay?" The sounds of Avalon blared through the speakers as an army of angry civilians moved in.

"Whatever you are isn't welcome here! Now put your hands in the air and step away from the car!"

Nirah turned in a slow circle, scanning the mob of angry people. Some part of this felt oddly familiar to how she felt on Avalon. All they needed was a golden gate to keep her out. All eyes suddenly turned toward Athena, who seemed to be flickering between car and dragon.

"Everyone, get back! There's another monster!"

Nirah threw her arms around Athena, sending a surge of light into her body. Her eyes flew open as two mighty wings solidified, along with shimmering scales and a fiery roar.

"Climb on my back!" Athena screamed as a rope flung through the crowd and wrapped around her.

"Look! I got the monster!" an angry voice screamed as another rope flew. "Someone help me get its feet!"

Nirah scrambled onto Athena's back, spotting the familiar kid from the alley wearing the same unicorn shirt. Their eyes locked as he pushed through the crowd and slid into the ring beside her.

"Are you following me? Who are you?!" Nirah screamed as another rope wrapped around Athena.

He spoke slow, drawn-out phrases as quickly as he could. "It's me, Uno. I figured you'd need some help."

"Uno! Boy, could we use one of your gates right about now!" Nirah smiled at the unicorn on his t-shirt. "I should have known it was you."

Athena attempted to flap her wings as another rope ensnared her. "A little help down here!"

Nirah's heartbeat sped up as Uno's slowed down. Before she could question what he was doing, he closed his eyes and took a nice, relaxing breath. She watched in awe as tiny specks of gold began to swirl around them, forming what looked like a gate of golden vines. The twisting vines grew taller as if reaching for the moon and allowed Athena the perfect moment to break free from the ropes.

She lifted towards the sky as the world below them faded. "Thanks, Uno!" Athena yelled while soaring towards the forest.

"That was incredible!" Nirah added as Uno plugged his nose.

"Oh, Nirah, your breath is horrible."

She sighed. "Well, that's because I stole dog pig powers."

Uno's eyes widened. "You stole dog pig powers? I bet they're so mad!"

She laughed. "Mad that I gave them a vacation from their stinky breath? Not likely."

Uno gasped. "You don't know what their powers do, do you?"

She shook her head. "Nope."

"All it takes is one deep, focused breath and you can inflate to the size of a house!" Uno laughed remembering the first time he saw the dog pigs do it. "They can grow like fifty feet tall, but when they exhale, boy, does it stink!" He could feel the wheels turning in Nirah's mind. "Promise me you won't use the powers unless you have to."

Nirah huffed. "I guess, but if those people hurt Sabik, even a little—"

Athena dipped between the pine trees and landed with a thud on a mountainous boulder. She sniffed the air and scanned the trees. "He's been here."

Nirah nervously rubbed the moonstone, remembering Vega's mention of the factory. *If only I knew what a factory was.*

Vega's voice swam into her mind like an echo. "See the two smokestacks coming out of the trees? That's the factory."

"Who are you?" Nirah asked the mysterious voice that kept popping into her mind. She waited another moment, then grew impatient. "At least tell me what you look like, so I don't mistake you for the enemy."

"The enemy?" Vega questioned. "Look, I know you're upset, but please don't hurt anybody. Okay?"

Nirah huffed. "I'll think about it, and I'll only ask you one more time. Tell me your name."

"Vega?" Barb's voice interrupted their connection but provided Nirah the answer she needed. "Are you sure you want me to drop you off at the lake? Why not just go in the side door like you did before?"

"Because I lucked out going in the side door before. At least this way I know there is a way inside."

"Aren't you scared what the water might do to you? What if you grow even bigger?"

Vega laughed. "I'm sure that serum wore off by now. I'm totally fine."

Barb drove as close as she could to the lake and parked. "And just where is this entrance anyway?"

Vega got out and scanned the forest. "There was a secret staircase somewhere around here."

"Well, where is it? Do you see it?" Barb called from the car.

Vega looked toward the lake. "Don't worry about me. I'll find a way in one way or another."

Barb laughed. "You're kidding, right? You're not seriously getting in there, are you?"

"Let's just say I'm getting an early start on my marine biology courses."

Barb laughed. "Suit yourself. In the meantime, I'll head to the main office, get what I can from the computers, and meet you right back here, okay?"

Vega waded out into the water and smiled. "Here goes nothing!"

Despite the green film on the top of the lake, the water below was actually crystal clear. Even stranger were the pillars of colorful crystal growing up from the bottom, which flickered as she swam over them. Suddenly, she realized it wasn't the crystals that were flickering but the tiny specks of light swimming around them. *Water fairies!*

The very thought of water fairies sent them scattering. *Wait!*

Vega swam as fast as she could, shocking even herself at how quickly she moved. Within seconds, she caught up to them and watched with wonder as the water fairies collected their powers and pushed a tiny, tortoise-shaped charm. She scanned the lake floor as her eyes grew wide. There were decades of personal items down here, mostly jewelry and trinkets.

Who did all this belong to?

The water fairies hurried towards what looked like a circular door at the bottom of the lake and swam in circles around it. With each rotation, more of the door was revealed, including the strange lock in the center.

She pressed her hand to the door, releasing what sounded like a big heavy lock behind it. Before she could think to react, the door swung open, sucking her inside. She flew through the darkness of the watery tunnel with only the lights of the fairies to guide her. Up ahead, the tunnel split, sending Vega one way and the water fairies another. All went dark as the tunnel ended, and the water drained into the floor.

"Don't freak out. Don't freak out." Vega said as four sets of glowing eyes lit up from the corners of the room. "Who's there?" she demanded.

The creatures stepped forward in unison. "We are the missing."

Vega's moonstone necklace glowed in their presence and cast a purplish light upon their faces. She gasped. "You're those kids…the ones from the posters. What are you doing in here?"

One of the girls stepped forward. "I'm Phoenix. That's Ember, Lumen, and May. Do you know what year it is?"

Vega scanned their eyes, which flickered between green and gold. "It's…2010." She squinted towards their faces. "That means you're probably around 18 years old now. You know, just based on what the posters said."

"There were posters?" Lumen asked, somewhat shocked.

"Of course there were posters. Four teens went missing," Vega answered.

"Four homeless teens," Ember added.

"Homeless or not, your lives matter. People are still looking for you."

Ember turned in a huff and walked away, dragging something heavy on the floor behind her. Vega squinted into the darkness.

"What…is that?"

Ember's eyes glowed with anger as she spun around. "Oh, you mean my tail?! It's the last thing to wear off once we get out of the water. Give it a few minutes and we'll look like you." She muttered to herself, "People are mad we don't look like them out there, and mad we don't look like them in here."

Vega rushed to her side, eager to console her.

"Look, I'm sorry for how people have treated you and for whatever happened to you."

"Not whatever. Whoever. The man that runs this place, he did this to us with his crazy experiments. His slimy green creation affected us all."

Vega was thankful it was dark in there; otherwise, they would have seen the shame on her face.

"Well, the good news is, I'm here to get you out."

Lumen laughed. "We know how to get out. It's the same way you just came in. The problem is leaving the lake. The green stuff on the water goes all crazy if you try to leave."

"Crazy, how?" Vega asked.

"Crazy like it gives you a tail. Hopefully you didn't get any on you."

"I was just swimming in the lake." She looked over her shoulder. "No tail that I can see."

"So, you're telling me that nothing has been different about you since you've touched the green stuff?" Lumen sounded almost annoyed about it.

Memories of every oddity flashed through Vega's mind. "Oh, you mean like breaking into a highly secured building, stealing a secret serum, and having a conversation with half-dinosaur people who live in the dark?"

Lumen laughed. "We don't live in the dark. We just prefer the lights to be off while we shift back into our human forms." He turned the lights on, revealing an oversized, state-of-the-art room with bunkbeds built into the walls, a small kitchen, and a giant window to the outside world.

"It's actually not so bad in here," May said while pouring a glass of water. "We have a roof over our heads, beds to sleep in, food to eat. It's just that sometimes, we turn into dinosaurs."

"That's not okay, May!" Lumen scolded. He looked at Vega, noticing her guilt-ridden face. "What's the matter with you? Why does your face look like that?"

Vega took a deep breath. "You know the guy with the wiry mustache in the white lab coat? He's my dad." She hurried to intercept their words. "Now, before you get mad at me, know that I had no idea about any of this until my friend went missing."

May took hold of Vega's hand. "I know who your dad is. He's the nervous guy that always spills stuff all over his coat. Sometimes, he mumbles to himself when he walks the hallways. I can't always hear what he's saying, only that he's upset."

The room seemed nearly airtight. "Hear him? How?" Vega asked.

May nodded towards the large rectangular vent. "Through there. Anyway, it's hard to be mad at him for his crazy inventions. Seems like he's trying to find a cure for cancer or something. And if he can cure cancer, then maybe he can cure our tails."

Lumen groaned. "Don't you get it, May? He's the one responsible for our tails. Every failed attempt at a cure got dumped into the lake and created that crazy algae."

Vega's eyes widened with every word they said. "Wait, what if not every experiment was a failure?" She reached into her pocket and pulled out the serum.

"What is that?" May asked.

"It's the serum I stole from my dad. He's been giving it to my stepmom, who until recently had cancer."

"Are you saying that vile of liquid is the cure for cancer?" May whispered.

Vega shrugged. "It could be the cure for a lot of things. Anyway, maybe it's the reason why I didn't have any side effects from touching the lake water."

May extended her hand. "Only one way to find out."

Vega handed her the serum. She took a single drop and then passed it to Lumen, who passed it to Phoenix and then Phoenix to Ember. Moments passed as they stood in silence, waiting for anything out of the ordinary to occur.

"Anything?" Vega asked.

May seemed to be the only one holding on to any hope. "No, but maybe it takes a while." She quickly scanned the room. "I think maybe for your sake you should get out of here—you know, in case we change into something else." She nodded towards the vent. "Since you don't have a tail, you can probably fit right through there."

Vega hoisted herself up onto the bunkbed, as the silver turtle charm fell out of her pocket. May hurried to pick it up.

"Hey! Where'd you find this?" She cradled it in her hands like a baby bird.

"In the lake, along with tons of other stuff."

May's eyes widened. "Ohhh, you must have been on the other side of the lake. We don't go over there."

Vega removed the cover to the vent and paused. "Why not?"

May laughed under her breath. "That's New Jersey Devil's side."

"You're kidding me?" Vega hoisted herself into the vent and looked back at May.

"Nope! And boy, is he scary. If you go back through the lake, stay away from that side."

Vega nodded. "Got it." She exhaled confidently. "Okay, I'm going to go find Sabik, free the others, and then I'll come back to check on you guys, okay?"

May climbed onto the bunkbed and accidently farted. She giggled. "Excuse me!"

Vega's eyes widened as May's hair suddenly began to grow into luxurious long golden locks. "Uh...May, what is happening to your hair?"

May combed her fingers through her glowing gold hair and held it in her arms like a baby. "I—I don't know. My hair never looked like this."

Vega smiled. "Well, if I need a rope to get out of here, I guess I know who to ask."

Both girls laughed. "But seriously, I'll be back for you as soon as I find Sabik and take down my dad."

"Wait," May insisted. "I know you might be mad at your dad for all of this, and don't get me wrong, he is very much responsible, but it's really the other guy you should worry about."

"What other guy?"

* * *

Barb crept through the garden surrounding the lab's corporate office. Everything about this place was pristine, from the spotless glass windows on the front of the building to the perfectly manicured garden around it. There were ornately sculpted bonsai trees, reflection pools, floating lilies, and a towering Onyx statue in the center.

"Who are you?" Barb whispered while circling the statue. "And why do you have three faces?" She pulled out her phone and snapped a picture, suddenly noticing the plaque at its feet.

Marici, goddess of illusion and invisibility.

"Speaking of invisible, there wasn't a person in sight, not in the garden, or the fancy glass building, either." She laughed to herself. "Unless everyone's invisible."

She hurried to the front door with keycard in hand. "Please work," she whispered under her breath as the door slid open. She hurried up the sleek marble stairs and down a long hallway with expensive oil paintings lining the walls. Her steps slowed as she stood before the painting of a white tiger. Its piercing green eyes were rich with color and stared into her soul. She placed her hand upon the canvas as a voice called out from behind.

"Are you Vega?"

A muscular Chinese man appeared at the end of the hall wearing a silk, green kimono.

Barb laughed. "She's quite popular these days. Sorry to say, I'm not her. Who are you?"

The man checked over his shoulder and ushered her towards another door at the end of the hall.

"You can call me Lan. Come, follow me. We need to get you out of here before he gets back." Lan pulled open the heavy door, revealing a bright white room behind it.

Barb shielded her eyes from the blinding lights and looked towards a table full of strange artifacts—tiger masks, bird feathers, tortoise shells, and a tank in the center of the room. "What kind of research company is this?"

Lan hurried around the table, collecting as many things as he could.

"The bad kind. Have you ever heard of the beasts of four directions?" He waited only a moment before continuing. "Associated with Chinese lore, they are considered the guardians of the universe. The white tiger of the west, black tortoise of the north, vermillion bird of the south, and azure dragon of the east. If one were to harness the powers of all four, they would be nearly unstoppable."

Barb peered into the seemingly empty fish tank. "So, this isn't about curing cancer?"

Lan looked confused. "What is cancer?"

Barb raised a questioning eyebrow. "Where are you from again?" Before he could answer, she raced towards the wall of computers. "Jackpot!" Her fingers went a mile a minute as she furiously input code. "Watch the door, will ya?"

His face seemed locked in a position of genuine shock as he stared at the computer. "What kind of monster is that?"

Barb laughed. "It's the best kind. Full of secrets ripe for the taking!" She pushed the thumb drive into the USB and watched as hundreds of files flashed upon the screen. "Let the data dump begin."

Lan's mouth hung open as he studied the screens. "What are you doing?"

"I'm downloading data from the servers. Servers are like giant systems with lots of information inside—information I'm copying onto my thumb drive." She smirked. "To put it simply, I'm collecting evidence."

She paused the download as something flashed upon the screen about bats. She skimmed the article and read aloud, "Merkel cells in bats linked to suppressing cancer. Scientists adding spider silk to stabilize protein."

"Where would they get that much spider silk?"

CHAPTER 10

Kick-Nut

Back in the police lab, Officer Height was busy analyzing the sticky green goo on the binoculars when the phone rang.

"Uh, huh. Wait, what do you mean a bear in a business suit?" She sighed. "I'll be right there." She set the phone down and hurried to the lab to grab the latest results. Her eyes scanned the page of foreign compounds. "Well, isn't that something?"

She picked up the phone and dialed. "Hey, Wendy, you got a second? You're not at work, are you?"

Wendy set the phone beside the bathroom sink and continued scrubbing her hands. "I am, but that's okay. What can I help you with?"

"Well, I don't really know what I'm looking at here and was hoping you could help me identify a compound."

Wendy pumped more soap onto her hands and tilted her head to hold the phone between her shoulder and ear. "Uh, sure."

"It's something I've never seen before. You know what, maybe I should just come to your office."

Wendy laughed nervously. "Sounds somewhat serious. Everything okay?"

Officer Height grabbed a few papers off her desk, grabbed her keys, and headed for the door.

"Stay put, Wendy, and whatever you do, don't touch anything that's green. Okay?" The green goo reappeared on Wendy's hands as a pink ball rolled into the bathroom.

"Why not?" she asked.

"Whatever it is seems to replicate whatever it touches. It's like it's alive or something. Anyway, just don't touch it."

Wendy carefully plucked the pink ball from the ground and slid it in her pocket. "Can this day get any weirder?"

* * *

Vega climbed through the maze of vents, immediately wondering if she'd made a mistake. She stopped for a second and attempted to listen to any indication of where in the building she might be.

"I'll never find him at this rate."

To her surprise, a familiar voice found hers. "Vega?"

She crawled towards the end of another shaft and looked through the grate, seeing only an empty dentist's chair and a large window that spanned floor to ceiling.

"Sabik! Is that you?" She scanned what appeared to be an empty room. "Where are you?"

"Over here."

"Over whe —" Vega gasped at the sight of her friend, hanging upside down in the chair. All but his face was invisible. It looked like his head was stuck inside of a glass bubble filled with fog.

"What have they done to you?!" She pushed the grate off and jumped into the room. Her hands gripped the sides of the glass bubble around his head. "Can I take this off?"

"Please! And once you're done with that, untie me from this chair!"

Vega scrambled around the chair untying him as fast as possible. "Everything is going to be okay. I'm here now, and I have that serum you told me to get. Which is crazy by the way!"

She immediately kicked herself for saying that last part.

He returned to solid form and shot a fiery glare her way. "What do you mean *that stuff is crazy*? You didn't try any, did you?"

Vega chuckled the guiltiest chuckle she'd ever chuckled. "No."

Sabik rolled his eyes. "Are you sure?"

She sighed. "Fine, if you really want to be all nitpicky, I only tried a drop. I only did it because I was in trouble and needed to escape Eddie."

Sabik pressed his ear to the wall and perked up. "Speaking of trouble. Someone's coming. Quick, take another drop of serum!"

"Are you crazy? There's no way I'm about to shrink myself down to the size of a gnat again!"

The footsteps grew closer. "Unless you want your dad to find out you are in here, you better take it. Now, this is super important. Whatever you envision is what you become. So, just imagine being invisible. No gnats."

Vega plopped a drop into her mouth and handed him the serum, of which he slurped down the rest.

"Did you just seriously drink that whole thing?"

He wiped his mouth with a satisfied grin. "I'm just taking back what they stole from me." His eyes narrowed. "Wait, why did you shrink into a gnat?"

"Beats me. I was just looking at my Midge playing card and—ohhh."

"Do you realize what this means? It means that you actually changed into the character on your playing card. You became Midge!"

The wheels in her mind churned at full speed. "So, if I imagine being her again, I will shrink into a feisty golden speck and have all the superpowers I assigned her?"

Sabik shrugged. "Probably, but fairy magic is a fickle thing." The footsteps from the hall closed in as Sabik quickly became invisible. "Whatever you're going to change into, you better do it fast."

Vega shrunk into a golden speck just as the door flew open, and in walked Officer Height. She looked like a bulldog as she entered the room—hands on her hips, eyes narrowed, eager to sniff out what she came for.

"Sabik? Are you here?" She strutted around the lab, assessing the strange set up. "Look, I'm just a regular police officer who's here to help you. So, if you are here, please, come out."

Vega fluttered above her head and headed back into the vent. Being in Midge form was incredible. She was everything she thought she would be: feisty, smart, and deeply connected with nature. In that moment, she could feel everything in the room, just as she had at Eddie's house, including the presence of others waiting outside in the forest.

Height shined her flashlight into the open vent. "Sabik, are you in there?" She was just about to hoist herself up on the chair and look inside when something else caught her attention—a strange shadow inching along the wall.

At first, it looked like a lizard, then a spider, and then a boy with wings. The shadow on the wall froze as she reached into her pocket and pulled out a chestnut.

"Now, look, there are some awfully weird things going on in this town—bears in business suits, stampedes of hamsters, dragons appearing on the boardwalk—but of all the places I could be right now, I'm here." She kicked the chestnut across the floor and waited.

It took every ounce of restraint to keep him from kicking it back to her. He looked at the nut and then at Vega, who emphatically shook her head.

"Well, let me tell you why I'm here. It's because I found something out about this place, and the people you were staying with. You know what I think? I think they took advantage of you. Lured you here because of what you are."

Sabik glared towards the vent, and then returned his attention to the chestnut.

"Now, I don't know what you are, but I know that you don't deserve to be locked up in here for someone to experiment on. Now, if you are here, please, just give me a sign."

He kicked the nut across the floor as her eyes lit up. "Sabik? Was that you?"

Vega sighed, triggering another flashlight shine towards the vent.

"Is someone else here?"

To make things even more uncomfortable, Nirah's voice suddenly popped into Vega's head.

"Hey, Vega. It's Nirah again. Are you in the factory?"

"Can't talk right now." Vega answered between clenched teeth.

"Is something wrong?" Nirah instinctually barked. "Something about you feels gross—like a fairy."

Vega remained silent.

"Anyway, did you find Sabik?"

"I did." Vega answered.

"Oh, thank goodness!"

"Where are you?" Vega whispered.

Nirah giggled. "Outside, and if you can't see me right now, just wait a few minutes."

"Uhhh, what do you mean by that?"

Nirah took a deep breath and slowly began to expand. True to the dog pig powers she had stolen, she began to inflate to the size of a house. She wobbled towards the building and peered her giant, pig-like face inside.

Sabik hurried to kick the chestnut towards Officer Height's feet, securing her attention.

"Look, Sabik, I don't have time to play games. This whole town is going crazy, and somehow, every wild animal in a hundred-mile radius has decided to gather outside this building, except for the bats. Those are still terrorizing the town every night. Go ahead, look outside—" she gasped at the sight of the sixty-foot pig glaring into the window.

"I've seen a lot of things in my day…" Her eyes began to flutter as her knees grew week. She collapsed, and just as she was about to hit the floor, two shimmering webs shot out from Sabik's fingers and caught her.

Sabik stared at his fingers as Vega flew a joyous circle around his head. "So, that's where you get it from!"

"Get what from? And can you stay put for a second? You're making me dizzy!"

Vega laughed. "That pink ball that's been bouncing around here. You know, the one that turns into a spider sometimes. She did the same exact thing!"

He looked genuinely confused. "I have no idea who you're talking about."

"Well, she's here, looking for you. I saw her in the solarium where the water fairies are."

"They have water fairies here?" A small tear trickled down his cheek, and as sadness overtook him, he began to flicker—first into the form of a boy, then a fairy, and then a crocodile. Vega's expression changed with him, committing it all to memory.

"Don't look at me like that." Sabik sneered the points of his teeth.

"Sorry, it's just that this is the most exciting thing this town has ever seen." Vega flew to the window and pointed. "Look!"

Sabik slithered to the window and looked below, spotting hundreds of animals who had gathered in his name—the black wolves, Arcturus bears, dog-pigs, hamsters, and a random stranger with a pink sports car.

"They're all here for you." Vega pressed her hands to the glass and tilted her head back, attempting to get a good look at the giant, hog-faced Nirah.

Suddenly, Wendy and a team of security guards barged into the room. "Sabik, stay where you are!" She looked at Officer Height, who was passed out, suspended in a rainbow-colored spider web. "What did you do to her?!"

As Wendy flailed her arms, the small pink ball fell out of her pocket and rolled across the floor. All eyes remained on the ball as it tremored, sprouted legs, and began to grow.

Vega flew around Sabik's head and whispered in his hear. "It's Neith!"

"Neith?" Sabik uttered the name he had only heard once before.

"Sabik?" Neith's bright-red eyes opened and locked on her son.

Vega's dad burst into the room and then ducked behind one of the guards.

"What in the world is that thing?!" Vega's dad shouted.

"This THING is the mother of the child you've been experimenting on. A mother who's come to bring him home."

"Mom?" Sabik uttered. "I thought you were dead!"

Neith kept her focus on the encroaching security guards. "Far from it." She scanned the eyes of the guilty. "Who here is responsible for capturing my son?"

Vega's dad took two shaky steps forward. "If you need to blame someone, blame me, but please, just let me explain."

Vega watched from above. As much as she wanted to materialize beside her dad, she knew that if she did so, she would lose her abilities in Midge form. With no serum left, it was safer to stay this way.

Before he could explain, Neith shot a web around his ankles and strung him up from the ceiling. "How does it feel to be held upside down? Doesn't feel too nice, does it?"

"Please! Let him go!" Vega plead.

"Let who go?" the sixty-foot inflatable pig boomed from outside.

The security guards shifted their attention between Neith and Nirah, unsure who posed the bigger threat—the angry mama spider or the giant inflatable pig that had grown taller than the building.

"Nirah?" Sabik mouthed from behind the glass.

She answered in a slow, drawn-out voice, "Get. Away. From. The. Wiiiiiinddoooooooooow."

Before he could wave her off or protest what was about to happen, she exhaled a big gust of stinky dog-pig breath and shattered the glass. Neith was quick to fire a pink web out the window and yelled, "Sabik, take hold of my web and go!"

In that moment, Sabik changed into something he'd never been before, a giant hard-shelled spider with the legs of a crocodile with a shimmering web that twinkled from his hands as he swung into the forest. He landed with a big springy bounce on the trampoline-like web as a wave of cheers resounded from below.

His eyes lit up at the sight of his friends—black wolves, bears, hamsters, dog-pigs, Athena, and Uno. Nirah, on the other hand, was still deflating back to normal size, and Neith and Vega were still inside the building.

"Sabik, what's the matter?" Uno asked.

Sabik slid down the web into the crowd. "My mom—she's alive!"

Gasps and unified cheers followed.

"Seems like you should be happy about that," Uno said. "Where is she?"

Sabik looked toward the shattered window. "In there, and she's really angry. I need to get her out of there before she does anything bad."

"I think I can help with that." Strands of gold swirled from Uno's fingers and grew like garden vines towards the open window. They inched up the side of the building and into the room.

"Everyone, stay here! I'll be right back!" Uno hurried into the building, past the front desk and up the stairs.

On the other side of the forest, Barb was sprinting, USB drive in hand, towards the factory. She raced inside, expecting to be stopped by a security guard or two, but to her surprise, no one was there. She hurried through the lobby and down a long hall lined with doors.

She yanked open each door as she passed, hoping to find Vega. She lingered in front of the last room, which was completely dark inside.

"Vega? Are you here?" She gasped as four pairs of yellow eyes greeted her.

"Uh, my name is Barb, and I'm assuming you're not Vega or Sabik." She took a step back into the hallway. The yellow eyes disappeared as the lights turned on, and a striking girl with long golden hair emerged. Behind her stood three abnormally blonde humans with radiant eyes and pale skin.

May stepped forward and greeted her. "We've seen your friend, Vega. She crawled through that vent and was trying to find Sabik."

Barb looked towards the vent and then opened the door a bit further. "Well, how about you guys leave through the door?"

Lumen reached a careful hand out into the hall and held it there as if waiting for something to happen. He smiled, pulled his arm back inside, and turned to face the others. For a moment Barb swore she saw a flash come from his eyes, that sounded like a camera shutter.

"Everything okay?" Barb asked.

Lumen smiled. "Just taking a mental picture of this moment." He looked to Ember and Phoenix, whose eyes looked the same. "Ready to get out of here?"

They followed him into the hall and waited for May, who seemed to hesitate in the doorway. "Are you sure it's okay?"

"Trust me, May," Lumen said as she hurried to join them. The blonde kids disappeared down the hall, leaving Barb alone in the room.

"Well, that was strange," Barb whispered to herself while eying the vent. She was about to jump up and have a look around when a loud crash came from down the hall followed by the golden flicker of a gnat-sized Vega flying straight towards her head.

"Vega? Is that you? You're a fairy again?" She sighed. "You really need to stop doing this. Where's Sabik?"

"Follow me!" Vega yelled.

She flew down the hall, ran up the stairs, and stopped in front of a room where Neith had every worker, including Vega's dad, strung upside down in a giant spiderweb. Barb peeked her head around the corner, spotted Neith, and ducked back into the hall. Silence followed.

Had she seen her?

The hairs on Barb's arms stood at attention as Neith slid into the hallway.

"Who are you?" Neith asked while sizing up the newcomer.

Her voice quivered as she answered, "B-b-barb. I'm Vega's friend. I think you know her..." Neith's ruby eyes narrowed in on her as she inched forward. "Uh, okay, so maybe you don't know her. In any case, I have information—stolen information that I took from this lab. Information that can help you."

Two venomous fangs poked from Neith's mouth. "What information is that?"

Barb reached a shaky hand into her pocket and pulled out the thumb drive. "They were taking people off the streets—people they didn't think anyone would realize were missing—and running experiments on them. They were trying to find a cure for cancer by using super cells from bats. These experiments had really bad side effects and turned some people into dogs, some into lizards, some into—"

"Enough!" Neith yelled. "What did they do to my boy?"

Barb looked towards the men dangling from the spiderweb, and suddenly, it all made sense. "Why didn't I see it before? Their original experiment wasn't working because they only had the bat cells, but when Sabik arrived, his body rejected the experiments because he had something that no one else did—spider DNA."

Neith leaned in, nearly eye-to-eye. "Go on."

Barb paced the room while rattling off her hypothesis. "Part of their study involved a special protein found in spider silk. The silk protein was needed to bond with the bat super cells and create what I understand to be a cure for cancer. The only part that doesn't make sense is the other stuff I found at the lab."

Neith suddenly looked suspicious. "What other stuff?"

Barb slid the thumb drive back in her pocket. "There was this room with different objects on the table—white tiger masks, feathers, a tortoise shell, and an empty tank in the center of the room. The man that was there said something about guardians—"

Neith's eyes widened. "What man? What did he say about the Guardians?"

Barb looked over Neith's shoulder and spotted Vega, who had latched onto a piece of the spiderweb. The tiny golden speck seemed ready to pull and unravel the whole thing. Even more alarming was the strange magical vines slinking across the floor towards Neith's feet.

"Uh, his name was Lan."

"Lan? As in Lan Caihe?"

Barb shrugged. "I don't know. He said something about harnessing the gifts of the four directions."

The magical vines began to interlock and grow behind Neith's back. Barb tried to keep her cool, but the sweat dripping down her forehead said otherwise.

"This man — the one who was trying to harness these powers. Where is he now?"

Barb shrugged. "I don't know."

Neith's fangs dripped with poison as she leaned in. "I sense a secret."

Vega's dad landed on the floor with a thud, and Neith spun around to face him. She looked at him and then at Barb.

"I guess you know my secret," Barb said with a forgivable grin.

Neith flung a handful of webs as the magical vines quickly formed a cage around her. "Let me out of here! I'm not the monster! They are!" Neith attempted to fling more webs, only to have them zapped.

Uno stepped into the room as Vega flew to meet Barb. She whispered in her ear, "You gotta get out of here!"

Barb looked at the remaining men suspended in the web. "Not without them! If you can you pull another thread loose, I can do the rest."

Vega flew as fast as she could toward the web, latched onto a thread and pulled. Barb jumped and grabbed it and gave one mighty tug, unraveling the rest. The men thudded to the floor one by one, angering Neith even more.

"What are you doing? They should pay for what they've done!"

Uno's hands glowed with magic as he stepped toward the cage. "This cage is for your own good. You did what you came here to do—free your son. Now, what do you say we head back to Avalon, together?"

Neith sighed. "You're right. I guess I got a little carried away. I'm just glad that he's safe."

Uno nodded toward the broken window. "Everyone is waiting outside for you. I'll let you out of here, but you have to promise that you won't web anybody else."

Neith nodded. "Fine. But, what about the people here? I mean, they've seen us now and heard about Avalon."

Uno sighed. "I agree that this is very unfortunate. I wish I had a way to fix it."

Vega flew towards Uno and landed on his shoulder. "I think I can help with that, but before I do..." She took off the moonstone necklace and handed it back to Neith. "This belongs to Sabik. Would you make sure that he gets it back?"

Neith nodded in appreciation. "Of course! And now we can use the moonstone to get us back to Avalon!"

"Wow, it really does that?" Vega asked.

Neith grinned. "It does. Among other things." She looked back towards the sleeping security guards. "Tell us about this idea you have."

"Well," Vega fluttered around the security guards as specks of magic fell over them, "one of my powers is erasing people's memories, and if they don't remember you or what happened here today, then they won't remember Avalon."

Uno hurried to let Neith out of her cage. "Come on. Let's go tell the others."

Neith flung a web out the window, wrapped her arm around Uno, and flew down to meet the others. Nirah was busy returning the powers to those she had stolen from, Sabik was wrapped in a spidery hug with his mom, and a pile of hamsters had climbed onto Athena's back. Vega watched from above as the animals climbed onto Athena, and the moonstone necklace began to glow.

Just as they were about to disappear, Vega sprinkled pixie dust on them, too, ensuring that when they got back to Avalon, they wouldn't remember her, this factory, or the things they had been through.

Once all minds had been erased and the beasts had returned to Avalon, Vega flew to Barb's house. She zipped through an opening in Barb's bedroom window just as she was getting ready to put the thumb drive in her computer.

"Vega? Is that you?" Barb's eyes danced around the room, chasing the golden flurry. "Hold still, will ya?"

As much as it pained her to do so, she knew she had to erase Barb's memory of the event, too. Barb was like a shark when it came to data, and once she uncovered one secret, it would lead down a deep and winding rabbit hole that could very well start things over again.

Barb did a girlish twirl as specks of gold rained around her. "What is this stuff?" She yawned and then quickly sat down at her computer. "Whew, I'm not feeling so…" She laid her head down on the desk and closed her eyes.

Vega flew back into the forest and landed beside the lake. She placed a finger to the water and grew back to normal size as two eyes rose from the water.

"Who are you?" Vega called to the monster, though she already knew its name. "You're the New Jersey Devil, aren't you?"

The dragon raised its head from the water as its golden eyes flickered.

"Well, I guess that's what we call you, but you probably have another name, don't you?"

The dragon smiled as its body disappeared, and only its eyes remained visible.

"How about I call you Transparent?" Vega asked.

The dragon winked just before disappearing completely.

"What a day," Vega said while walking the gravel trail towards home, where Alice was outside waiting.

That night at the dinner table, Vega's eyes remained on the one empty chair.

"Something the matter?" Alice said before finishing the last piece of gnocchi.

Vega gazed across the table, noticing how radiant and happy Alice looked.

"No, I just had a long day." Vega took one more bite and carried her plate to the sink. "Mind if I turn in early? I'm exhausted."

Wes joined her in an oversized yawn. "Me, too! Man, I don't know what's come over me, but I'm drained."

Vega silently smirked before heading upstairs to bed. That night, as she slept, something itty bitty fluttered into the room, a guest, from far, far away, who came to ensure Avalon's secrets remained intact.

Florenza sprinkled a wave of pixie dust over the sleeping girl, dipped out the window, and flew back to the stars.

* * *

Vega rolled over, coming face-to-face with her ringing phone.

"Hello?"

"Vega? Hey, it's Barb. I had the craziest dream last night! You were in it!"

Vega stretched while eying the open window. "Oh, yeah? What was it?"

She could feel Barb's excitement through the phone. "It was crazy! There was this madman that was trying to become a superhero, and his name was Cancerian. He was born in a lab or something and had become unstoppable."

Vega laughed. "Cool! I'll draw him as a playing card."

Barb suddenly seemed a bit more serious. "Wanna know the weird part?"

Vega smiled. "That wasn't the weird part?"

Barb exhaled. "When I woke up this morning, there was a thumb drive in my room, and it doesn't belong to me. I mean it is one of mine, but there are things on it that I didn't put there."

"What kind of things?'

"Come over to my house. I'll show you."

www.ingramcontent.com/pod-product-compliance
Lightning Source LLC
Chambersburg PA
CBHW022036170626
46808CB00003B/1224